Hi

Leighann Dobbs

This is a work of fiction.

None of it is real. All names, places, and events are products of the author's imagination. Any resemblance to real names, places, or events are purely coincidental, and should not be construed as being real.

Chapter One

Kate Diamond grabbed a flute of champagne from the silver-rimmed tray before the waiter whisked it off into the well-dressed crowd. Raising the sparkling glass to her lips, she took a sip, her nose twitching slightly from the bubbles as she scanned the elegant ballroom at the swanky Crowne Point Hotel for her target.

Her heart skipped when she caught her own reflection in the large wall-sized mirror at the end of the room. Lavender eyes blinked at her from underneath platinum hair that had been piled high on her head and secured with a glittery rhinestone comb. Her strapless gown—in silver satin to match her elbow-length gloves— glittered with various shaped rhinestones that studded the bodice. A small matching purse dangled from her wrist. She hardly recognized herself ... and hopefully, neither would anyone else.

Shifting her gaze over to the bar, her lips curled into a soft smile as she spotted the object of her search—Julian Crowder. In Kate's small circle, Julian was known as "The Crow"—partly because of his name, partly because of his fondness for shiny gemstones and partly because of his ability to fly above any type of criminal prosecution resulting from his nefarious activities as a go-between in the black market world of stolen art, artifacts and gemstones. He didn't actually steal any of the items himself. He simply connected the thieves with stolen objects to buyers who didn't mind acquiring those stolen objects.

Julian knew everything there was to know about the most recent jewel robberies and possessed information about a certain gemstone ... information that Kate would stop at nothing to get. Looking down, she adjusted the bodice of her gown so it showed off her ample assets and started across the ballroom toward him.

She silently cursed the way the tight fitting floor-length dress hampered her stride as she elbowed her way slowly through the sea of gowned and tuxedoed patrons gathered for the local Artist Guild charity event.

As she moved along the crowd, the latest brands of expensive perfume—Chanel, Patou, Clive Christian, and Hermes—stung her nose and made her lungs ache. She pushed a momentary pang of nausea aside and let the din of voices fade to the background as she studied Crowder.

Like most of the men in attendance, he was dressed in a black tuxedo and crisp white shirt. He sat with his tall bar chair swung to the side, one elbow leaning on the bar, his round stomach sticking out like a pregnant penguin. The lock of dirty blond hair he'd combed over to hide his receding hairline hung across his forehead into his eyes as he tilted his head upwards to appraise the young woman who was unfortunate enough to be standing at the bar next to him. She was tall and beautiful, a model perhaps, and Crowder would have had to tilt his head backward at an uncomfortable angle to look at her face.

But, he wasn't looking at her face.

As Kate closed in on her quarry, she watched him raise a crystal tumbler of amber liquid to his lips. A glint of light from the gigantic diamond on his pinky ring almost blinded Kate as she slid up to the bar in-between Crowder and the model.

Pushing her now empty champagne glass across the bar for the bartender to fill, she turned her head toward Crowder and favored him with her most flirtatious smile. Crowder was a rich man, reputed to have a voracious appetite ... for both food and women ... the latter of which Kate planned to use to her advantage.

"Hi." Kate contemplated batting her eyelashes but figured that would be overkill.

"Well, there sure are a lot of pretty ladies that support the Artist's Guild auction here." Crowder's gaze drifted from Kate's face to her cleavage.

"Oh, I love the arts." Kate took the full champagne glass from the bartender, raised it to her lips and took a big gulp, then giggled. "I also love the champagne ... although I might have had a teensy bit too much."

Kate pretended to stumble into Crowder who put his hand on her waist to steady her.

"Ooops." Kate giggled again.

"I don't believe we've met." Crowder studied her with black, birdlike eyes.

"We haven't," Kate said holding her hand out to him. "I'm Tempest Rochfield."

Crowder's right brow raised a fraction of an inch. "Any relation to Bernie Rochfield?"

Bernie Rochfield was a well-known art collector and reputed to be one of the richest men on the planet. Kate figured her being a relative would pique Crowder's interest in her even more.

"A distant cousin." Kate nodded her head, then hiccoughed and giggled again.

"Julian Crowder." Crowder extended his right hand while managing to keep his left possessively on her waist. Kate fought to keep a seductive smile on her face as she suffered through his lingering sweaty, limp handshake.

Finally, Crowder withdrew his hand. Kate took another gulp of champagne, and then started to fan herself with her free hand.

"Phew ... it's awfully stuffy in here." She looked around the ballroom, then turned her attention back to Crowder leaning in closer to him. "So many people. Don't you think it's a bit crowded?"

Crowder's sweat-glistened face turned pink and Kate recognized the predatory look in his eye. He put his hand over hers suggestively. Kate felt a surge of triumph battle with a wave of revulsion as he leaned in to whisper in her ear.

"We could go somewhere less crowded," he suggested.

Kate felt impatience lap at her stomach—she had him just where she wanted him, but she didn't want to blow it by moving too fast or making it seem too easy for him. She pulled back from him, plastering a wide-eyed look of innocence on her face.

"Why Mr. Crowder, I don't know about that ... I mean ... we just met." She batted at his arm playfully with her small purse.

Crowder played along. Leaning closer again, he tried to persuade her by pretending like it was an innocent invitation. "Why Miss Rochfield ... I hope you don't think—"

Kate pretended to listen as he droned on. She'd give him a good five minutes of resistance and then let him think his powers of persuasion had won her over. That way he'd be more worked up and distracted, making it easier for her to complete her mission.

Her gaze drifted across the room as Crowder tried to sweet talk her. It was packed full. Waiters circled the crowd with trays of drinks and appetizers. People had gathered in groups, talking, drinking and having a good time. Except for one lone man, who stood off to the edge, scanning the crowd.

Alarm shot through her when she recognized him—Ace Mason.

What was he doing here?

Kate wondered if the FBI agent was here for the same reason she was. No, it was impossible—no one else knew Crowder's connection to the theft of the giant ruby. Still Mason's presence here was unnerving. She turned her head away from him—she couldn't risk him recognizing her. She needed to speed up her plan and get Crowder out of there *now*.

"—assure you I meant only a brief respite to avoid the crowds and talk about art." Crowder was saying.

"Well, of course you did, silly." Kate smiled down at him while watching Mason out of the corner of her eye. "That sounds lovely."

Kate tilted her head toward the exit and Crowder bolted up out of his seat nearly sending it toppling over. Kate turned and walked in the opposite direction of where Mason was patrolling the crowd. Crowder followed close behind her with his hand on the small of her back.

Wishing she could walk faster, Kate cursed her tight skirt again as she sashayed toward the French glass doors that led to the hotel elevators. Just as they got to the doors, her eyes met Mason's in the mirror—her heart kicked. Did she see a glimmer of recognition on his face?

A quick look back told her she must have been mistaken—Mason had returned his attention to the crowd.

Kate let out a sigh of relief as she sailed out the door and headed toward the elevator. She tried not to jerk back as Crowder brushed his arm against her breasts in his pretense of leaning over to push the elevator button. "I'm on the sixth floor."

"I love the view from the sixth," she said as the doors opened and he pushed her in.

Inside the elevator, she giggled as she stumbled against him. She noticed Crowder's hand slipped from the small of her back to cup her bottom and she prayed the elevator would get to his floor quickly as she snuggled against him.

He turned toward her, his hot breath fluttering against her cheek as he leaned closer. Her nose wrinkled at the smell of stale garlic and whiskey. Panic nipped at her as his face hovered inches from hers. The thought of him kissing her was revolting—but she'd do it if she had to in order to keep up the charade ...

Ding!

Mercifully, the elevator doors opened and Kate stepped out from his grasp causing him to stumble forward.

"We're here!" she announced cheerfully as she wiggled out into the hallway. Crowder rushed to catch up to her, fumbling for his key as he steered her toward his room.

He stopped in front of the door to room six forty-two. Every one of Kate's nerves was on high-alert. It was almost ShowTime.

She rubbed herself against him as he put the card in the door. He turned to look at her and she smiled, giving him her most seductive look. His eyes glittered with understanding as he pushed the door open.

Kate was barely inside when he slammed it closed and turned around, trapping her against the wall. His hands pawed at her, pulling her closer. She shuddered in revulsion as his lips touched her neck. Crowder must have mistaken the shudder for something else and his hands roamed to her breasts.

Kate giggled. "Not so fast." She wriggled out of his grasp, then grabbed onto the end of his tie and pulled him backward into the room toward the bed. Dodging his advances so as to avoid his lips meeting with hers, she spun him around, pushed him down on the bed, hiked up her tight dress and straddled him.

"Oh you like to be on top? That works for me." Crowder tried pulling down the top of her dress but Kate swatted his hands away.

"Not yet, you bad boy," she said playfully as she reached for the purse that was still dangling from her wrist. Crowder lay obediently on the bed, his breathing growing heavy with anticipation of what was to come ... or at least what he *thought* was to come.

Kate pulled a tiny perfume vial from her bag and pulled out an old fashioned dauber, using it to dab a little perfume on the hollow of her throat.

"A little for me, and a little for you," she bent over and brought the perfume dauber to his neck. Crowder grunted, his eyes drawn to her cleavage—he didn't suspect a thing.

Kate pushed the end of the dauber and a tiny needle slid out. She pierced the skin on Crowder's neck and pushed the bulb on the end injecting him with the liquid hidden inside the vial.

He jerked his eyes from her cleavage to her face, his brows forming in an angry V. "Hey what the—"

But Crowder didn't finish the sentence. He was fast asleep.

***

Forty-five minutes later, Kate pulled one of the pillowcases off the king size pillow on the bed. She reached down and yanked at the bottom half of her gown, which pulled away to reveal black spandex pants she wore underneath.

Contorting her arms around to her back, she unzipped the top of the gown and slid it off. She flipped it inside out to reveal the black lining. Two pieces that had been tucked into her bra fell out—they were sewn on to the front of the bodice, then draped over her shoulders and attached to the back with eyehooks to form sleeves. She zipped the zipper on the front, transforming the top into a black vest.

Looking in the mirror, she grabbed the top of her hairdo and yanked. The platinum wig flew off and copper curls tumbled down around her face. She shoved the wig into the pillowcase along with the bottom of her dress and headed into the bathroom.

Squinting into the mirror, she jabbed her finger into her right eye and pulled out the lavender contact, then repeated the process for her left, blinking twice at her own amber eyes that stared back at her. She threw the contacts into the toilet and flushed.

A loud snore from the bed sent a jolt of adrenaline through her. Pivoting on her heels, she raced back into the bedroom.

Was Crowder waking up?

Kate checked the hotel room clock. No, it was too soon. Gideon said the dose in the vial would knock him out for at least five hours. She looked at the bed. Crowder was curled up, his face buried in one of the pillows. Fast asleep.

Even so, Kate didn't want to linger. She sat on the edge of the bed and pulled off her shoe, snapping the temporary stiletto heel off to reveal a much lower kitten heel underneath. She did the same with her other shoe, then threw the heels into the pillowcase before turning her small purse inside out and pulling out straps that transformed it into a black fanny pack that secured around her waist. She slipped the perfume vial inside and took one last glance around the room to make sure everything was exactly as it had been when she arrived.

Everything was in place, right down to the computer she'd been on for the last forty-five minutes copying data. She cast one last glance at Crowder asleep on the bed. If what Gideon said about the serum she injected him with were true, he'd wake up sometime in the early morning with a whopping headache and no memory of what happened during the hours before he fell asleep. If they were lucky, he wouldn't remember meeting her, much less taking her to his room. But even if he did, he'd never be able to connect the silver gowned platinum blonde to Kate.

Grabbing her USB drive from the computer table, she slipped it into her bra, blew Crowder a kiss, then peeked out into the hallway to make sure it was empty before slipping out the door with the full pillowcase in hand.

She hurried toward the north end of the hallway, where she knew from previous research that she'd find the trash chute. Pulling the metal lid open, she shoved the pillowcase down, then peeled off the long gloves and tossed them in after it. She closed the door using her elbow—she'd removed the gloves last for a reason, and it wouldn't do to screw up and leave a fingerprint now.

She turned and walked back toward the elevator, tapping the button with her knuckle. Basking in the glow of self-satisfaction she always felt after a successfully completed job, she tugged on her platinum and cubic zirconia earring and whispered, "Mission accomplished ... I have the data."

A voice crackled in her ear. "Excellent. Bring it to home base."

Chapter Two

"Home base" was the twelfth floor of the Meridian building that housed the famous *Ritzholdt Museum*. Kate worked for the Ritzholdt ... well, for the business that owned the Ritzholdt, along with dozens of other famous museums. She reported directly to the head honcho, Maximilian Forbes, whose office she was now making a beeline for.

As she raced down the corridor, hope swelled in her chest. Hope that the elusive CEO would actually be in his office. Surely, he would want to be here to see this important information in person. After all, what else would he be doing at one-thirty in the morning?

She skidded to a halt just inside his outer office, her eyes narrowing at the obstacle in her way—Mercedes LaChance, Forbes' assistant.

"Is he in?" Kate peered around the petite brunette trying to get a glimpse into Forbes' inner office.

"Mr. Forbes is busy." Mercedes stood, hands on hips, blocking the thick oak doors that led to his office. "You can wait here," she said gesturing to a contemporary white leather and chrome sofa that sat facing her desk.

Kate glared at the antagonistic assistant, cursing her bad luck that she would be here at this time of night.

Didn't the girl have anything better to do?

"I have important information he's expecting," Kate said in her haughtiest tone.

Mercedes looked down her perfectly shaped nose at Kate, which was a feat in itself since Kate was a good foot taller.

"Yes, I know all about it," Mercedes said. "Gideon is in there now ... you will be shown in when Mr. Forbes is ready." She gestured to the couch again.

Kate let out a sigh and flopped on the sofa, the leather creaking grudgingly as she sat. Despite working for Maximilian Forbes for almost a year, Kate had never actually *seen* the man. Not that she hadn't tried. In fact, it had become kind of an obsession with her—she was dying to know if the man was as gorgeous as his voice sounded.

Kate had gotten most of her communication from Max over the phone, through email, text messages, Skype text chats and one time even by carrier pigeon. Just thinking about the deep, masculine timbre of his voice made her feel all tingly. And it didn't hurt that he had a touch of an Irish accent ... or was it English? Either way, the sound of his voice made Kate melt. She wondered if he'd have that effect on her in person. But something always came up whenever they were supposed to meet. Kate was beginning to wonder if Maximilian Forbes even existed.

The big oak door opened and Kate's heart jumped—tonight might finally be the night. She leaped up from her seat, feeling slightly disappointed that the figure in the door was Gideon Crenshaw and not Max Forbes.

"Is he ready to see me?" Kate started toward the door.

"What?" Gideon glanced back into the office and Kate followed his gaze. Except for the large mahogany desk, matching filing cabinets and a Monet painting on the wall, the office was empty.

Kate's hopes deflated. "Where is he?"

"Oh, Max?" Gideon took her elbow, steering her away from the office. "He had to run out but I told him about the great job you did and he said to tell you he's very pleased."

Kate stared at Gideon who was not only a co-worker but also a good friend. To say he was a geek was to put it mildly. He even looked the part with curly brown hair that often stuck out at odd angles from running his hands through it when figuring out complex calculations for some gadget or formula.

Kate glanced down at his sweater vest. Hadn't she advised him not to wear those anymore? Then back up at round black-rimmed eyeglasses with such thick layers of glass his light green eyes appeared enormous. Gideon was responsible for all the cool gadgets Kate used on her "assignments" including the serum she'd given to Crowder as well as the perfume vial hypodermic she used to inject it. She loved the guy to pieces and didn't want to hurt his feelings, but right now she wanted to catch a glimpse of Max.

"But he *was* in there with you," she said peering back over her shoulder.

"Yeah. He took his private elevator down to the garage." Gideon gave Kate a sympathetic look—he knew she'd been trying to catch a glimpse of Forbes since she came to work there. "You'll never catch up with him. Besides you might not want him to see you in that outfit ..."

Kate looked down at the skimpy black vest and tight spandex pants she'd forgotten she was wearing. As the head insurance investigator for the Ritzholdt, she usually wore something more business-like in the office. Tonight, she hadn't had much choice. The pants were the only things that would fit undetected under the gown and Gideon had designed the top of the gown to turn into the vest. She'd been too excited about getting the information from Crowder's computer to change before coming here. Maybe it was a blessing in disguise that Max had to run off.

Kate puffed out her cheeks and turned back around. "Right. Well, I guess there's plenty of time for me to talk to him later," she said glancing sideways at Mercedes who was now sitting behind her desk with a smug look on her face.

She fished the USB drive out of her bra as she followed Gideon out into the hall.

"I was able to get all the data from the computer," she said holding out the tiny device.

"Great." Gideon snatched the drive from her hand and hit the button for the elevator. "So, the serum and hypodermic worked, then?"

"Like a champ." Kate followed Gideon into the elevator and watched him press the button for the basement. "He's probably still sleeping."

"Excellent." Gideon held the USB drive up to his eye. "Now let's see if this baby can tell us just what Julian Crowder plans to do with the world's largest ruby."

***

The world's largest ruby crystal, otherwise known as "The Millennia Ruby", had been stolen from the *Ritzholdt Museum* several weeks earlier. Which was no easy task considering it weighed almost nine pounds and was the size of Kate's hand.

The crystal was reputed to be the largest raw ruby crystal ever dug out of a mine and had been donated to the museum by the mine owner, Xavier Badeau. In its raw form it was worth millions, but cut into individual stones it might be worth even more.

"Do you think Crowder will sell the ruby whole or have it cut?" Kate asked Gideon, who was huddled over his computer tapping furiously at the keys.

"I don't know." Gideon paused his tapping and squinted up at her, adjusting his glasses on his nose. "For a collector, I think the unique value would be in getting it whole. There's not another one as large, even though it's a raw unpolished crystal. Once it's cut up, it loses a lot of the appeal, I think—I mean—anyone can buy a big ruby."

"Sure, but the Millennia might yield a very large stone, or several, that could be more valuable cut and polished than the raw crystal," Kate pointed out.

"Yeah, but these are collectors we're talking about. They already have lots of money. What floats their boat is getting their hands on something that no one else has," Gideon said turning back to the computer.

"Even if it means they have to keep it hidden away." Kate sank down into a chair and slid it next to Gideon's pet dachshund, Daisy, who was curled up in another chair. She absently stroked the dog's silky fur. Gideon was the best at what he did and Max did whatever it would take to keep him happy—including letting him keep his dog in the lab. Of course, it worked in Max's favor too; since Gideon didn't have to leave the lab to tend to the dog, he could work more hours.

While Gideon focused his attention on the computer, Kate looked around the room. Hidden deep in the basement Gideon's lab was gigantic, encompassing most of the entire floor. In the middle were long stainless steel tables, like the one Gideon's computer sat on. Around the perimeter were glass windowed rooms—each one contained some strange tool or contraption that Gideon was developing. Some had the window shades open so you could see in, others were closed tight and Kate knew that's where his top-secret developments were.

Kate stifled a yawn and sank further into her chair wondering how Gideon managed to stay so alert at this ungodly hour. She guessed it had something to do with the pile of Red Bull cans on the table beside him.

She contemplated going home to bed, but she *had* to know what Gideon found on the computer since the information would dictate her next move. Kate thought about what she might have to do to get the ruby back. Although she held the mundane title of "Insurance Investigator", the actual mechanics of her job were much more exciting. She did what the police were often unable to do—got back items stolen from the museum by whatever means possible.

Sure, the police always *tried* to catch the thieves, but the truth was, one often had to react quickly and use unorthodox methods to catch thieves at their own game and the police weren't known for doing either of these. Kate should know—she used to be in law enforcement.

But now, Kate loved working for the museum. She had an amazing amount of resources, the latest technology and, thanks to Gideon, innovative contraptions to help her do her job—things she never had when she worked for the FBI. Plus, Max trusted her and gave her free reign to do whatever it took to retrieve the items. Not only that, but her job often took her to exotic locations ... and the generous expense account didn't hurt either.

Of course, there *was* the little problem of operating outside the law at times. But Max's money and resources had been able to get her out of any of the scrapes she'd gotten into and, since she was usually just retrieving items stolen from them in the first place, she wasn't really doing anything *too* illegal—most of the time.

Kate wondered if operating on the outskirts of the law added to the excitement for her. It did have a certain appeal, except for when she had to dodge the law, like last night when she'd had to dodge FBI agent Ace Mason.

Kate pushed thoughts of Ace Mason out of her head. Even if he was on the case of the missing ruby he certainly wouldn't have the information she did. The FBI was too slow and bloated to gather the intel this fast. She had nothing to worry about.

Closing her eyes, she tried to think of where the trail would take her. Crowder was known to hold auctions and parties in strange and exotic locations. He'd do whatever it took to attract his buyers and help them maintain their anonymity. Maybe she'd jet to Europe, go on an exotic cruise, or bask on a Caribbean island. After she recovered the ruby, she could take some extra vacation time to enjoy herself.

Kate could almost smell the salty, tropical sea air and feel the gritty sand under her feet as she pictured herself sipping a pineapple and rum-laced umbrella drink and gazing out onto the aqua ocean while the sun warmed her skin ...

"Kate ... Kate ..." Kate heard Gideon calling from far away. She slowly opened one eye.

Had she fallen asleep? She must have because Gideon was shaking her shoulder to wake her.

"Wha—?" she mumbled sleepily.

"I've got it!" Gideon pointed excitedly to the computer screen and Kate sat up in her chair, leaning over to see what the excitement was about. "I've figured out where Crowder is going to try to sell off the ruby."

"Really?" Kate perked up, fully awake now. In her mind, she started sorting through her closet, choosing from her summer wardrobe. She'd have to bring that cute turquoise sundress ... the salmon colored shorts set ... she might have to buy some new sandals. She couldn't wait to get away. The weather was turning cold in Boston and a tropical location was just what she needed.

"Come on Gideon, tell me where it is." Kate looked from the computer monitor to Gideon as she squirmed in her seat. From the look of excitement on her friend's face, she knew it was someplace good.

"This is a chance of a lifetime, Kate," Gideon said. His obvious excitement was infectious. She perched on the edge of her seat, waiting for him to announce the location.

"You're going to Antarctica."

Chapter Three

"Antarctica?" Kate stared at Gideon trying to determine if he was kidding. "But there's nothing there except snow and ice."

"... And Emperor penguins, Minke whales and Weddell seals among some of the most amazing sights on the planet," Gideon replied. "If you get the chance you should kayak up to the icebergs—they're spectacular. And you *must* swim in one of the lagoons at Deception Island."

Kate eyed the pile of Red Bull cans and wondered if drinking too much of it could cause delusions. "Swim? That sounds cold. Isn't the water frozen there?"

Gideon looked at her as if *she* was the one who had gone crazy. "Of course not. Deception Island is an active underwater volcano with geothermal lakes and lagoons. It's like lounging in a hot tub. Oh, and Deception is loaded with chinstrap penguins so take your camera. I'd love some pictures of the Emperor penguins too, if you have a chance—it's very hard to get pictures of them."

"You're joking, right?" Kate said hopefully. "The ruby can't really be in Antarctica ... there's nowhere to keep it."

"*Au contraire.*" Gideon tapped the keys on his keyboard. "I'm not joking and there *is* a place to keep the ruby—an ice hotel."

"Ice hotel?" Kate shivered as images of her suitcase full of bathing suits and sundresses turned to ski pants and parkas.

"Yeah, you know, a hotel built entirely out of ice and snow." Gideon turned his monitor toward her to reveal a series of pictures of what looked like the inside of a giant igloo, except much fancier. "Like the famous one in Sweden."

Kate scrunched her face at the monitor. "I do remember hearing about that but I didn't know there was one in Antarctica."

"That's the beauty of it ... no one does." Gideon tapped on the keyboard again and a satellite photo appeared showing a snow-covered image. He pointed at a dark rectangle in the middle of the image. "According to the data on the USB drive you gave me, Crowder had one built in the most remote place he could think of. It's brilliant really. A perfect way to keep anyone from knowing who his guests are since no one else would be anywhere near."

" … And he has the ruby there." Kate said it as a statement rather than a question.

"Among other things. It looks like he plans to have some sort of auction for the ruby, some jewels allegedly from Katherine the Great, a Matisse, a Van Gogh, and a few other items that can't be sold through public, legal channels."

"And once the auction is over, all he has to do is melt the hotel and the evidence vanishes," Kate said.

"Exactly. It's brilliant!"

"Must be expensive to build."

"Oh, it is. But Crowder has money and the commission he'll make from getting buyers for the stolen goods …" Gideon let his voice trail off. They both knew it would be in the millions.

"And just how am I supposed to get into this ice palace and get the ruby out?" Kate asked.

Gideon pressed his lips together. "It's not going to be easy. The guest list is by invitation only. The event is for two days, ending in the auction."

"Two days?" Kate stared at Gideon. "You mean people actually sleep in an ice hotel?"

"Yes, it's very comfortable actually," Gideon said as if he'd done it before, which made Kate wonder if he had. "You don't sleep on ice. The rooms come equipped with specially heated sleeping bags on top of down-filled mattresses."

"Great." Kate tried unsuccessfully to muster some enthusiasm.

"It will be fun. It's the warm season there right there now so it's only about fifteen degrees inside the hotel. I'll make sure you have the latest thermal clothing. I think I can dig up some gloves and socks for you to take—they're heated with a special chemical, shake them and they stay warm for 24 hours. Not too many people can say they slept in Antarctica." Gideon looked at the computer screen wistfully. "To tell you the truth, I'm pretty jealous. I wish I could go, but I have to stay here and man the fort."

Kate's heart pinched. She was always jetting off to exotic locations and Gideon never got to go anywhere.

"Sorry, Gid," Kate said, vowing to adjust her attitude and appreciate the opportunity to go somewhere unique. "I wish you could come too."

Gideon rummaged in one of the thin drawers that slid out from under the table, retrieved a box of Tic-Tac's and held it out to her. Kate frowned at the box before taking it. *Was her breath that bad?* She blew out on her palm to test it.

Gideon laughed. "That's actually a camera." He opened one side of the Tic-Tac box to reveal three buttons. "This button zooms, and this one controls the shutter to snap the picture. It takes great pictures and if you press this button on the bottom, it will take pictures of beams of light from lasers, just in case you need to map out the lights on a security system." He demonstrated how to work the camera and handed it back to her. "Oh, and there's actually Tic-Tac's on the other side."

Kate studied the device, taking a shot of Gideon before slipping it into her pocket.

"I was hoping that since I can't go, you could take some pictures of penguins and other wildlife for me. Antarctica is actually teeming with unusual creatures."

Kate sighed, wondering when she'd find the time—or inclination—to go outside and take pictures of wildlife. Then she saw the hopeful look on her friend's face. It was the least she could do. How hard could it be to snap a few pictures of penguins?

"Sure, I'll do my best," Kate said, then turned the conversation back to business. "Okay, so how do I get an invitation to this thing?"

"We'll leave that up to Max. He always seems to be able to come through in that area. With all his connections on both sides of the law, I'm sure he'll be able to finagle something."

"And I'll need transportation that can get me there … and something that I can sneak the ruby out in."

"Right, I thought you'd never ask about that." Gideon got up from his chair and walked over to one of the glass windows. "I've been working on this."

Kate craned her neck to see what was in the room. It looked like some sort of souped-up motorcycle. It was a little wider than a regular bike, with a dome windshield that came up over the rider's head. Instead of wheels it had a wide studded belt and there where what looked like wings folded up on the side.

"Don't tell me that thing flies." Kate felt a twinge in her chest. She certainly hoped Gideon didn't expect her to fly it.

"No, it's a ski-cycle … and it floats!" Gideon punched some numbers into the keypad beside the door and it slid open with a hiss. Stepping into the room, he motioned for Kate to join him. "Come on, I'll show you how it works."

Kate got out of her chair and stretched. Daisy did the same, and then followed Kate into the room where Gideon was fiddling with some switches and dials on the dashboard of the ski-cycle.

"As you can see, it's built like a motorcycle, but it has the belt that goes across snow and ice —like a snowmobile. The bullet-proof windshield helps to protect you—and a bulletproof shield slides up in back." Gideon pressed a button and a Plexiglass shield slid up from the back of the seat. "Of course you only want to use that if you are being shot at, otherwise the drag will slow you down."

"What are these things?" Kate pointed to the pieces folded up on the side.

"Ah!" Gideon ran around to the front of the bike. "That's the beauty of this baby." He pressed a button on the dashboard and the pieces unfolded making a V shaped hull that extended from the middle of the tires underneath the bike. "It turns into a boat, so if you're assailant is chasing you on land, you can drive right into the water and leave him in your dust."

Kate nodded. "Impressive."

"Oh, and the best part?" Gideon flicked a switch and Kate saw the belt start to move. "It's completely silent, so you can make your getaway without anyone knowing."

"That's perfect. So, all I have to do is figure out how to steal the ruby, and then jump on this cycle and ride off to ... where?" Kate scrunched her face at Gideon.

Gideon waved his hand dismissively. "That's one of the details that needs to be worked out. Assuming Max can get you an invite, I figure the best thing is to have someone waiting in a boat. Cruise ships and yachts are not uncommon in the waters there, so no one will be suspicious of a boat trolling around the water. Then you'll need an accomplice to bring the cycle to you once you've secured the ruby. If you're lucky, no one will be the wiser, and the two of you can make a quick getaway and be safe on the boat before Crowder even knows the ruby is gone."

"You make it sound so easy," Kate said.

"Well, it can be if you get the right people to help. You'll just need a cruise ship or yacht and someone who can drive it. Plus, someone who doesn't mind speeding across the Antarctic snow at ungodly speeds." Gideon grinned at her. "Oh, and your accomplices should be good at evasive maneuvers, be crack shots and have nerves of steel."

"Well, if that's all," Kate said, "then I think I know just the people to help."

Chapter Four

Kate parked her rental car in the parking lot of the *Golden Capers Beach and Yacht Club*. Jumping out, she stretched, turned her face to the sky and let the Florida sun warm her face.

Her flip-flops slapped against her heels as she walked over to the fence that hid the community pool from sight. For once, her five-foot-seven height was an advantage and she only had to stand on her tiptoes slightly to see over the top of the wooden fence, which was ringed with plastic party lights.

Empty lounge chairs in turquoise and lime green surrounded the pool. The aqua-hued water winked at her in the sunlight. Two large stainless steel barbecues sat on either side of a grass Tiki Hut bar. Kate could see the remnants of last night's (or was it this morning's?) drinks in blenders that sat atop the bar.

"Kate!"

Kate looked up to see her mother leaning over the second floor balcony. Carlotta Diamond was an exotic beauty that looked twenty years younger than her age of sixty-eight. Looking up at her mother's tanned face, wide smile and thick chestnut hair piled high on her head, Kate sighed, wishing for the millionth time that she'd inherited her mother's good looks.

"Hi Mom," Kate shaded her eyes from the sun, "Where is everybody?"

"Probably sleeping it off." Carlotta spoke with only the slightest hint of Italian accent as she gestured excitedly toward the open door of her condo. "Come on up!"

Kate sidestepped a small brown gecko that skittered out of her way as she skirted the edge of the pool. Reaching the stairs, she stopped for a second to marvel at the bright red flowers of a hibiscus shrub that ran the length of the building. Beyond the shrub, she could see the clear waters of Lemon Bay.

She grabbed the wooden banister and started up the steps of the Spanish style stucco building that housed half the condos belonging to that *Golden Capers Beach and Yacht Club*—the most unusual retirement resort that Kate had ever heard of.

Most people would have never thought *Golden Capers* to be unusual. It certainly *looked* like any other Florida retirement community. Made up of two buildings set in an 'L' shape with a pool in the center, it had Lemon Bay in the

42

back and the Atlantic Ocean across the street in the front. The people were just your normal everyday retirees ... on the surface.

What most people didn't know about *Golden Capers* was it was filled with ex-thieves and con men. Not just your garden variety, either—the real pros in the field. The ones that had been wildly successful and retired *before* they got caught.

Kate's parents were no exception—her mother had been a jewel thief, her father a legendary con man who planned hundreds of successful heists. The place was filled with retired folks who all had unique talents—lock pickers, explosive experts, masters of disguise. Kate had known most of them since she was a child and they were like family to her. That's how she'd picked up most of the skills that had made her successful in the FBI—she'd been schooled by the best and her unique knowledge on how the criminal mind works gave her an edge in catching the bad guys. Now that she worked for the *Ritzholdt*, the knowledge and resources were invaluable.

They weren't bad people, really—most of them wouldn't hurt a flea. Of course, the people they stole from might not see it that way, but that had been long ago. Now, they'd pooled their resources to buy the retirement complex and they all lived on the right side of the law—most of the time.

The people at *Golden Capers* were really just like any of the other senior citizens in Florida except they had special knowledge ... knowledge about art, antiquities and gemstones as well as knowledge of how to get into and out of any type of secured environment. And, of course, they also knew how to use evasive maneuvers if they were being chased and were expert shots, which was the main reason why Kate was there.

Kate tapped on the open condo door and Carlotta whirled around from her task of arranging grapes on a platter. She ran to Kate, her arms wide. Kate bent down to hug her mother, who was almost a foot shorter. Her heart flooded with warmth as Carlotta returned the hug and pecked a kiss on both of Kate's cheeks. The scent of her perfume—Chanel No. 5 —flooded Kate's nostrils, stirring up happy memories of childhood.

"It's wonderful to see you." Carlotta held Kate at arm's length. "You look great."

"Thanks Mom, so do you," Kate said truthfully—somehow Carlotta managed to looked better with each passing year. Even the thin strands of silver that had worked their way into her hair made her more attractive.

Carlotta's almond-shaped deep brown eyes twinkled with excitement as she pulled Kate further into the condo. "I'm dying to hear about your new assignment."

Carlotta let go of Kate and swooped up the platter with the grapes. Balancing it in one hand, she grabbed a pink liquid filled pitcher with the other. "But, I'm sure you're hungry from your long flight so I figured we could snack out on the lanai."

"I sure am." Kate reached out to relieve her mother of the pitcher, then picked a grape off the tray and popped it into her mouth while she followed Carlotta past the breakfast bar and through the contemporary style living room toward a wall of sliding glass doors that opened onto the lanai.

The lanai was a twenty-foot wide balcony that ran the entire length of the condo. The view of Lemon Bay was breathtaking. The table had already been set with small plates and glasses. The two women pulled out seats and settled in.

Kate took a deep breath of salt-spiced ocean air and let it out slowly. Glancing out toward the peaceful blue waters of the bay, she felt a sense of calm.

"It's so great to be here," Kate said talking not only about the scenery but also about being with her parents. She didn't get down here nearly enough and loved spending time with them ... especially if that time included thinking up ways to retrieve pieces for the museum.

Carlotta nodded while she nibbled a grape. "Your father and I love it. So peaceful and relaxing."

A gentle warm breeze ruffled Kate's hair as she looked out at a small sailboat that was navigating the channel leading to the open ocean.

"Lemonade?" Carlotta held up the pitcher.

"Love some," Kate said. She grabbed some grapes, crackers and cheese from the platter as her mother poured the lemonade.

"Where's Dad?" Kate peered back into the condo just as she heard a door slide open from behind her.

"Oh, I'm right here, Kitten." Vic Diamond came onto the lanai fresh from a shower and rubbing his hair with a towel. Like her mother, he looked much younger than his age. Even though his dark hair was now mostly gray, his tall, muscular frame and tanned skin gave him a youthful appearance. *The stress-free active lifestyle must agree with them*, Kate thought.

"I had a big tennis match today ... had to shower up." He leaned down and pecked Kate's cheek before settling himself into a chair.

Carlotta pushed the tray of grapes toward him and he picked a few off.

"It's great to see you Kate, but I know you didn't come here *just* to see us." Vic leaned across the table, a sparkle of excitement in his eyes. "Tell us about this new job and how we can help."

Kate's parents listened intently while she told them about the Millennia Ruby and how it would be auctioned off at the ice hotel.

"So you're going to steal it back?" Vic narrowed his eyes at Kate. "Is that legal?"

"Well, technically, the ruby belongs to us, so taking it back really isn't stealing." Kate nibbled on the corner of a cracker. "Besides, what's Crowder going to do? Call the police on us?"

Vic and Carlotta laughed.

"But surely, the museum has the police looking for it ..." Vic said.

"Yeah, of course. But we all know how slow they are," Kate answered. "They'll probably still be looking for it in Boston by the time I've gone to Antarctica and come all the way back."

Carlotta's brows shot up. "True. They always were pretty slow on the uptake."

"That's why Max has sent me in to look for it. He knows I'll actually get it back—the police are only added insurance, just in case. We don't want them to feel left out if it turns out we really need them," Kate said.

"But this sounds like a tough job." Vic's eyes turned dark with concern. "How will you get in ... and out? Do you know anything about the security? Is your boss providing you with a good cover?"

"That's why I've come here for help," Kate said. "I know you guys are the best."

"Boy, I'd like to get my hands on that ruby," Carlotta said teasingly, then quickly added, "just to see it, not to *steal* it. You know I'm out of that business and besides, I prefer my gems to be cut and polished and set into gold or platinum."

Kate narrowed her eyes at her mother. "I hope you're not thinking of coming with me."

"Well, now that you mention it, that's not such a bad idea." Carlotta looked at Vic who nodded. "You're going to need backup ..."

Vic must have seen the look on Kate's face because he held his hands out to stop the two women from arguing before she could get her mouth open.

"Let's see what we're up against first," he said standing up. "Then we'll know exactly who we need to send in and where to place them."

Kate watched her father duck back into the condo and come out with a notepad, pencil and laptop computer. He sat back down at the table, pushed the pad and paper over to Carlotta and then opened the laptop.

"This will give me a chance to use my new software," Vic said as he tapped on the keyboard.

"They have software for planning heists now?" Kate asked in disbelief.

"Not everyone does, but since we have our very own software geek right here at *Golden Capers, we* do," Vic said, then at Kate's look of alarm he winked and added, "We don't use it to plan real jobs but we do like to keep our skills sharp and it's fun to play around with."

Carlotta leaned forward, her eyes glittering with excitement. "Okay, spill all the details about the auction."

Carlotta scribbled in the notepad and Vic tapped on the keyboard while Kate told them about the ice hotel and the special auction.

"Did you say your young man had satellite photos?" Vic asked without looking up from the computer.

"Young man?" Kate's forehead creased. "Oh, you mean Gideon? He's not *my* young man."

Kate saw her parents share a look.

"That's too bad. You should find someone to share your life with," Carlotta said. "It's wonderful when you find the right person."

Kate's heart warmed at the affectionate look her parents gave each other as Vic covered Carlotta's delicate hand with his. She felt a wistful tug—would *she* ever find love like that?

"I thought maybe that other FBI detective—"

Kate held her hand up to stop her mother from saying more. She didn't like the way the conversation had turned. She was still angry about what had happened thirteen months ago— angry with *both* the FBI and the *other* detective her mother was referring to.

She felt her chest tighten as she thought about the case that had ended her otherwise stellar FBI career. She'd singlehandedly captured one of the most notorious thieves in

FBI history and how had the FBI thanked her? By firing her. Sure, she'd had to use some unorthodox methods to catch the guy, but she didn't think it warranted her getting *fired*. And in the end the bad guy, Damien Darkstone, had been released from jail on a technicality thanks to the *other* FBI agent, Ace Mason.

"Let's not talk about *that*. He wasn't the right one and I have no desire to take up with anyone else right now."

"That's right Kate," Vic said. "Don't settle, especially for a young yahoo FBI detective."

Kate nodded at her father, he'd never trusted Kate's old partner and, as Kate eventually found out, with good reason.

"Oh, well, you're not getting any younger." Carlotta looked at Kate out of the corner of her eye. "Benny's son is single again if you want us to fix you up ..."

"Bangkok Benny?" Kate scrunched her face picturing the rotund man she knew as "Uncle Benny"—short, balding and overweight, she imagined his son looking much the same. "Umm ... no thanks. Why do you call him Bangkok Benny anyway?"

Carlotta and Vic exchanged another look and they both started laughing.

"Oh, just something that happened on a job in Bangkok when we were younger." Carlotta blushed. "It really wouldn't be appropriate for us to say."

"Okay." Kate let it go ... the less she knew about her parents' previous life the better and judging by the look on her mother's face *this* was something she definitely didn't want to know. "So, back to my job ..."

"Yeah, can you get Gideon to email the photos?" Vic asked. "I can input them into this program and it might help us figure out how to get the ruby out of there."

"Sure, I'll text him your email address." Kate picked up her phone and tapped out a text to Gideon.

A few seconds later, her phone vibrated on the table and Vic's computer pinged.

"Got it!" Vic hunched over the computer typing and working the mouse. Then he sat back staring at the screen and rubbing his chin with his thumb. "It looks like the hotel is about five miles from ocean. We'll have to either fly you out or find a way to get you to the ocean and pick you up in a boat."

"Actually Gideon has part of that covered." Kate described the ski-cycle to her parents.

"That sounds interesting … but you can't just carry that with you," Carlotta said. "So we'll need someone on the ground—or in a boat—to bring it to you."

Vic glanced over at the dock that extended out into Lemon Bay where several yachts were moored. "A few of the folks here keep their yachts over there, but I'm not sure one is strong enough for the Antarctic environment … or if we could even sail it there in time."

Kate's phone vibrated and she picked it up to read the text. "Looks like I have an answer for that. Max has a small cruise ship that was retrofitted from an old research vessel—it has ice-strength hulls and all the comforts of a cruise ship … *and* it just happens to be in the Antarctic. We can borrow it for the job."

Carlotta clapped her hands together. "That's perfect. We can combine work with a pleasure cruise and help Kate all at the same time!"

"Uhh … I'm not sure it will be a pleasure cruise, Mom," Kate said. "It will probably be dangerous and I doubt it comes staffed."

"Pfft … *you'll* be the one in the most danger. We'll just be on the boat providing backup." Carlotta turned to Vic. "Now, all we need to do is figure out how to get Kate in and out of there …

and how she can steal the ruby without getting caught."

***

It was getting dark by the time they'd finally come up with a viable plan. Kate sat back in her chair, a tickle of nervousness spreading in her belly as she watched the pelicans dive head-first into the waters of the bay for their dinner.

Would the plan work?

After several texts back and forth between Kate and Gideon—and even a few from Max—they'd worked out the resources and personnel they'd need. Max knew from previous jobs that Kate had access to people with unusual skill sets and he was all for recruiting them. Kate often wondered whether this easy access was what had prompted Max to offer her the job.

Vic's software had been able to determine the layout of the ice hotel and even figure out a little about their security.

Uncle Benny would help her with getting around the internal security—that was his area of expertise. Gideon was sending down a package, which would include a covert communications system where Kate and Benny could send and receive messages. It was assumed that any communication going in or out of the ice hotel would be strictly monitored, but Gideon just happened to have some nifty gadgets that would communicate in code. Kate could give Benny more information on the security once she got inside. She was actually pretty good at disarming security systems herself, but the extra help couldn't hurt.

They'd even recruited an old friend to captain the ship and their old getaway driver, Sal, to drive the ski-cycle.

Everyone they'd contacted to help was agreeable—eager even. Of course, they were paid well for their efforts, but no one at *Golden Capers* needed the money. They all loved the opportunity for adventure, which let them make use of the skills they'd spent their entire lives honing. The adventure came with minimal risk ... unless you counted getting shot at risky, which most of her parents' friends didn't.

Max was working on getting Kate an invite as well as an alternate identity through his vast underground network. The cruise-ship-turned-research-vessel was already en route to a safe place where it could rendezvous with a helicopter carrying Kate's backup team, which, against Kate's wishes, included her parents.

Gideon had already loaded the ski-cycle on the helicopter and was sending a care package with the necessary gadgets and some self-heating clothing down to Kate.

Everything was running smoothly and Kate didn't know whether to feel nervous or elated. This was the biggest job Max had ever asked her to do and she wanted to prove to him, the FBI, and maybe even herself, that she was good enough to pull it off.

Kate's phone vibrated on the table signaling another text. Her throat tightened as she read it.

Sucking her bottom lip between her front teeth, she looked up at her father. "How long do you think it will take to pull this all together?"

Vic shrugged. "We're all retired and looking for something to do so it shouldn't take too long. Why?

"According to this text ... I leave for Antarctica tomorrow."

Chapter Five

The ice hotel rose out of the snow covered ground like a gigantic igloo. The two story high front was constructed out of two-foot wide ice blocks that sparkled in the sun like oversized ice cubes. Above that, a roof of snow sloped down to form the sides of the hotel.

The double doors—made from real glass, not ice—opened and Kate did a double-take at her reflection as her white fur boots carried her inside. Her hair, now a sleek jet-black color, had been pulled into a tight chignon at the nape of her neck. Her dark eyes peeked out from underneath an ermine fur hat, which matched the hood and cuffs of her snow-white jacket.

The hotel lobby had an inviting aqua glow, even if it was a bit cave-like. The cathedral-like walls sloped upwards to a peak at the top. Along the sides were rows of round ice columns. The lobby furniture was made from ice and there was even an ice chandelier hanging from the very center of the room.

Julian Crowder glided forward to meet her in a snowsuit that resembled a tuxedo. Kate almost laughed out loud. The outfit made him look like an overstuffed penguin instead of giving him the suave, sophisticated impression he was probably hoping for.

"Ahh ... Miss Hunt. So lovely to make your acquaintance." He took Kate's outstretched hand, which was clad in white leather edged with ermine, but instead of shaking it, he bowed over it brushing his lips against the glove.

"What? No hot chocolate or whiskey to greet me after that horrendous journey?" Kate snapped, jerking her hand back. Normally she was never rude, but she was undercover, assuming the identity of Chyna Hunt, the reclusive granddaughter of the even more reclusive multi-billionaire Lucien Hunt. Chyna Hunt was also an avid wildlife photographer, but known to be a diva and Kate had to play the part ... although she had to admit it wasn't too hard to be rude to Crowder.

"But of course." Crowder gestured to the ice sofa where one of the staff, clad in all black thermal wear, much like what Kate had on underneath her jacket, was placing a steaming cup of something. "Have a seat and Fritz will take your bags to your room."

And search them thoroughly, Kate thought, as she walked over to the ice sofa. The thought of them going through her bags didn't faze her—a casual inspection would reveal nothing that would give her away.

The sofa's seat was covered with a furry animal hide. Kate sat down, surprised at how comfortable it was. She found herself wondering if divots melted into the couch from the body heat as people sat there.

Picking up the steaming mug, she sniffed. The velvety smell of chocolate spiced her nose. Her taste buds detected a bit of cinnamon and brandy.

"Delicious."

"I'm glad you like it." Crowder slipped onto the sofa across from her. "So, what piece is your grandfather interested in?"

Kate waved her hand in the air. "Oh, you know his tastes are varied. He's simply instructed me to procure whatever I can at a good price."

"And what might a *good price* be for each item?" Crowder asked.

Kate pasted a fake smile on her face and leaned toward him. "Well now, if I told you that it would spoil all the fun, wouldn't it?"

Crowder chuckled leaning back in his seat, his hawk-like eyes drilling into Kate's as she sipped from her teacup without dropping eye contact.

"Mr. Crowder?" Crowder looked in the direction of Fritz's voice and raised his brow a fraction of an inch at Fritz.

"Ms. Hunt's room is ready." Fritz bowed and backed away.

Crowder stood. "Would you like to freshen up?"

"Absolutely, I'm exhausted after the arduous trek to this godforsaken place." Kate took one last sip of hot chocolate, placed the teacup on the table and stood.

"This way," Crowder said holding out his elbow, which Kate took reluctantly. "Take an hour or two to freshen up, then I will give you and some of the other guests a tour of the pieces we'll have on auction."

Crowder stopped in front of a wooden door, which was set in an ice frame and checked his watch. "Say, five p.m.?"

"That sounds fine," Kate said. Turning to the door, she felt Crowder's eyes drilling into the back of her neck. She turned back around. "Is something wrong?"

"No. I was just wondering if we'd met before ... you seem familiar." Crowder stared at her with furrowed brows.

"I don't think so," Kate said, the corners of her lips curling up in a mischievous smile. "I *do* have one of those familiar faces."

Crowder nodded and pushed the door open for Kate who slipped inside, shut the door and locked it noisily behind her.

***

Kate collapsed against the door, a whoosh of air puffing out her cheeks. Pretending to be someone else could be a lot of fun, but it was also a lot of work, especially when one was operating on hardly any sleep.

Kate eyed the animal-skin covered bed, surprised at how comfortable it looked. She walked over and pressed on it expecting it to be as hard and cold as a block of ice. Instead, the bed yielded to the pressure of her hand. It was warm. Inspecting it closer, she saw there was a thick down mattress on top of the block of ice that worked as the box spring. The mattress was covered with a heated sleeping bag, which had the animal skins thrown on top.

Maybe sleeping here wouldn't be as bad as she thought. But not right now—she had to check out the room first.

Looking around, she realized it was quite cozy. Not big, but big enough to house a bed, nightstand, table and chair—made out of ice, of course. The ceiling was domed giving it a comfortable, cave-like feeling. One wall had a fireplace carved into the snow with red lights at the base to imitate fire.

Kate unzipped her parka and pressed a button on the clasp of the string of white Akoya pearls that hung on her neck. The button was a homing beacon that would transmit the coordinates of her exact location to the ship, where they would overlay the coordinates onto the satellite photo of the ice hotel in order to determine where, exactly, her room was. This would help them come up with a getaway plan and make sure the getaway vehicle would be right where she needed it.

Next, she scanned the entire surface of the room for bugs, cameras—anything they might be using to spy on her or see what was going on in the room. She found nothing.

Turning her attention to her luggage, she unzipped her one suitcase, flipped the lid open and bent down eye level with the surface of the case. The monofilament fishing line she'd laid across had been disturbed, indicating that someone had opened the case. But she'd expected that and there was nothing inside that would give away her charade ... not at first glance anyway.

Kate pulled a mirror out of the suitcase and studied her reflection, congratulating herself on her disguise. The black wig looked natural, as well it should since it was the best money could buy, made from real human hair. The blue eye shadow, heavily applied just the way the reclusive Chyna Hunt wore it, offset the contacts, which were dark as coal—both to match the color of Chyna's eyes and also to enable Gideon to fit them with a special coating that allowed Kate better night vision.

Putting down the mirror, Kate fought off a tremor of nervousness. Crowder had thought she looked familiar. She didn't think he'd figure out that she was the blonde at the hotel, but she'd be smart not to interact with him too much. She wondered if any of the other guests knew Chyna. She certainly hoped not, they'd be sure to see through her disguise. But Gideon's research had indicated that none did and she trusted him implicitly.

Kate glanced again at the bed, her eyelids growing heavy. She wasn't just acting when she'd told Crowder she'd had a tiring day. The travel itinerary to get to the ice hotel was exhausting. First, she flew in a private jet to a remote airport near Antarctica where she was ushered into a helicopter that flew her to a boat in the South Atlantic Ocean that sailed her to the edge of a glacier where she hopped on a shuttle boat that ferried her to the glacier where she met the snow bus that took her to the ice hotel. Crowder didn't provide directions to the hotel itself—probably to keep the exact location secret—so guests were told to meet the helicopter at specific times. The private jet for the first leg of the trip had been supplied by Max to help keep up the charade as the wealthy heiress.

Kate stripped off her parka, removed the pearl necklace and matching earrings, and then wiggled into the sleeping bag, snuggling into the down mattress. She set her watch for four thirty —that would give her a couple of hours of much needed sleep before her next performance as Chyna Hunt.

The warmth enveloping her body had a relaxing effect. The snow dampened any sounds from the rest of the hotel. Kate burrowed into the down mattress, threw the animal fur blanket over herself and fell into a deep, restful sleep.

Chapter Six

The beeping of the alarm on Kate's watch interrupted her dream. The same dream she'd had over and over for the past year. The one where the director of the FBI was asking for her badge and gun.

Kate eagerly opened her eyes and shook off the last vestiges of sleep. She hated that dream.

Crawling out of the sleeping bag, she stood and stretched, then checked herself in the mirror. Wig still on straight, makeup not smudged. Perfect. She pulled out the self-heating gloves and socks that Gideon had sent and shook them up to activate, then slipped them on.

Slipping the pearls over her neck and threading the matching pearl stud earrings through her pierced ears, she grabbed a black fur cape and threw it over her shoulders. The cape, her black ribbed turtleneck and black thermal pants along with the heated gloves and socks should keep her plenty warm while still looking somewhat fashionable. She slipped on her fur-lined boots and headed out to the shared bathroom before meeting the others.

Kate emerged from the bathroom refreshed and ready for the night's activities. The hotel was small with only one corridor, so she didn't have to do any guesswork to figure out where she'd find the rest of the guests.

Seven people milled around in the icy lobby, six she'd never seen and Crowder. Kate didn't know if the six had arrived while she'd been sleeping or had already been there relaxing in their rooms. The thick snow-packed walls of the hotel had acted as soundproofing and she'd heard nothing while she slept.

Kate plastered a disinterested smile on her face as she approached the group.

"Ahhh, Miss Hunt." Crowder turned to her. "I trust you slept well?"

"Like a baby," Kate said.

"Good. Then let me introduce you to everyone else." Crowder tugged on her elbow, pulling her closer to the crowd. "Everyone, this is Chyna Hunt."

Conversation stopped and everyone turned to Kate who tried to smile while remaining aloof. Not only was that what the real Chyna Hunt would have done, but she also didn't want to encourage any friendships. The less she talked to anyone the better.

"Mr. and Mrs. Palmer Powell." Crowder gestured toward an older couple who stood close together. The woman appraised Kate critically. The man didn't seem interested in her at all. Kate smiled and nodded.

"Ms. Carmen DeLuca." Crowder pulled Kate toward a thirty-five-ish woman with long caramel colored hair and eyes to match who was bundled in a pure white snowsuit. She narrowed her eyes at Kate, but stuck out her heavily gloved hand for a limp and noncommittal handshake.

Crowder turned to the next person in line. An elderly man, hunched over with a cane and clear plastic tubing running from an oxygen tank at his side to both nostrils. "Mr. Jon Nguyen."

The old man let out a long, dry wheeze as he bowed his head at Kate who returned the greeting.

"And this is Mr. White." Crowder nodded toward an incredibly tall albino who stared at Kate without making any move to greet her.

Kate suppressed a shiver and turned to the last man—average height, average hair, average eyes, the man was almost invisible and certainly very forgettable.

"This is Simon," Crowder said.

As Kate shook Simon's hand, she realized it was no mistake that he was so average looking. He was most likely a hired hand, sent to bid on behalf of a collector who wanted to remain anonymous.

Looking down the row of people, she realized any of them could be hired hands. Maybe none of them were the real collectors. For all she knew, all of the names were fake. She didn't really care one way or the other, but she knew Crowder must know the real names or who was behind them. Surely, he would have checked them out before letting them attend.

They stood silent in the lobby for a few uncomfortable seconds, sizing each other up. Then Crowder broke the silence.

"Shall we go view the items?"

***

The room where the items were being held was at the opposite end of the hotel from the bedrooms. Crowder led the way, stopping at the glass door of a room that appeared pitch black inside ... except for the crisscross of bright red laser lights.

So, the security system did use laser tripwires, Kate thought as she felt her heartbeat speed up. Scanning the sides of the door and walls, she wondered what other systems he had in place as she slipped the box of Tic-Tac's from her pocket.

Crowder nodded to the six-foot ten-inch giant guarding the door and he punched some numbers into a keypad causing the lasers to switch off and lights to come on illuminating the room. Crowder opened the door and ushered them inside.

Kate hung back, making sure she was the last to enter so she could get a good look at the door. Just as she suspected, a thin red wire ran from the bottom, up the side and into the snow packed wall where the hinges were attached. It was wired to an alarm system which, thanks to Uncle Benny's expert training when she was a kid, would be a piece of cake for her to disarm.

The room was awash in light. Ice columns, pedestals and mirrors reflected the beams from the overhead lighting, making it seem even brighter than it would normally have been.

Kate saw several paintings hanging on the snowy walls, their backs protected by animal hides. One she recognized as a Picasso that had been stolen from a wealthy patron of the Ritzholdt last year. She wondered briefly if she should steal it back for them. No, better to stick to the original plan; carrying a four-foot painting on the ski-cycle might be a problem.

Kate's attention was drawn to the center of the room where Mrs. Powell was bending at the waist to inspect a jeweled crown inside a glass case. But it wasn't the crown Kate was looking at; it was the item beside it—the Millennia Ruby.

It sat on a pedestal, inside a clear box. The transparent red hues were even more gorgeous with the lighting here then they'd been in the museum. Maybe Max should think about adding ice and snow to his display?

Kate inconspicuously aimed the Tic-Tac box at the ruby and tapped on the side.

"Uh-hmm." Crowder cleared his throat to catch their attention. "We'll start over here."

Everyone walked over to the corner where Crowder was standing in front of a brilliantly colored painting. A Monet? Or was it Manet? Kate always got them confused, but it didn't really matter. She had little interest in the painting—she was too busy scoping out the room in order to determine what, exactly, Crowder had for security.

As Crowder droned on about the painting, Kate searched the floor and ceiling areas out of the corner of her eye.

He moved to the next painting, which gave Kate a chance to change her position and look at a different part of the room.

Crowder made his way through all the items that would be offered in the auction, saying a little bit about each one. Kate feigned interest, nodding and murmuring with the rest of them, while she secretly used the time to familiarize herself with the layout and search for hidden security cameras or other security devices. She didn't find any—could the laser tripwire system be the only security? That seemed too good to be true.

Finally, the tour was over and they were back at the door. Kate hung back, maneuvering herself so that she'd be the last one out of the room.

"Oh, and in case you are wondering," Crowder said as they filed through the door. "We have minimal security here. Just the locked door and the lasers. But don't let that tempt you—if you did happen to make it out of here, there would be nowhere for you to go."

Crowder scanned the crowd with his black, beady eyes. "But none of us here are thieves are we?"

They all laughed and Crowder gave the signal to the giant who turned off the light. The laser beams flicked on and Kate held out her box of Tic-Tac's with the camera lens pointing to the room.

"Mint?" she asked no one in particular.

A few of them held out their hands and Kate tapped the little white oval mints into them, taking each opportunity to also click a picture of the laser beams.

"And now ... I do believe dinner is served." Crowder waved his hands in the direction of the lobby and the crowd followed him down the hall.

***

The dining room was in an alcove next to the lobby. Kate wasn't surprised to discover the long table was made of ice. She had to admit it *was* pretty. Little white lights inside the ice ran along the sides of the table giving it a subtle inner glow. Ice chairs covered in animal skins sat around the table.

They took their seats, Crowder at one end and Mr. Powell at the other. Kate ended up in-between Mrs. Powell and Mr. White, with Simon across from her. Carmen sat on one side of Simon and Mr. Nguyen on the other. Kate couldn't help but feel a tug of worry at his red face and heavy breathing.

"We specialize in collecting mostly art pieces," Mrs. Powell was saying as one of the staff placed steaming bowls of soup in front of each of them. "What do you collect?"

Kate's stomach tightened as she looked at the older woman. She'd studied the dossier on Chyna Hunt and her grandfather and knew enough to discuss their collecting habits in general, but if anyone asked specifics, she might get tripped up. "I'm mostly a jewel and pearl collector." Kate glanced down at the necklace she wore. "My grandfather is the one interested in this auction, though."

"Oh, and what might he be interested in?" Carmen cocked an eyebrow at Kate from her spot at the end of the table.

Kate slapped a smug smile on her face. "Well, now I really don't want to say. Considering you all might be competitors in the auction."

Beside her, Mr. White laughed and Kate turned her head to meet his red-eyed gaze. His pale skin was almost translucent.

"I think we all know your grandfather has a taste for the unusual," he said.

Kate didn't reply, she just tilted her head in response, and then focused on her soup. She ladled the silver spoon into the brown broth, stirring up a chunk of carrot, celery and a piece of light meat. Chicken? She took a taste. No, rabbit. It was delicious and, judging by the slurping sounds coming from everyone else, Kate wasn't the only one who thought so.

The conversation turned to discussion of the favorite piece in each person's collection and then to some of the more famous stolen art, artifacts and jewels as they made their way through courses of venison, greens with strawberries and finally a crème brûlée. Kate wondered how they had cooked such a fantastic meal—did the ice hotel have a full kitchen hidden somewhere, complete with ovens and stoves?

Kate noticed most of the others had their wine glasses filled many times while she nursed her one glass. She kept quiet, thankful she could act the part of the stuck-up recluse and no one would find it odd.

Jon Nguyen stood as the plates were being cleared. He coughed several times and then sucked in a wheezy lungful of air.

"Gentlemen, Ladies." He bowed in the direction of the table. "I'm an old man in need of lots of rest and the day has been tiring. I hope you will excuse me after this most excellent meal."

Crowder stood. "But of course, I hope you have a restful night."

Nguyen nodded again, turned and left, dragging his oxygen tank after him.

Glad that Nguyen had broken the ice, Kate tossed her napkin on the table and stood. "And I must also retire to my room. I want to take advantage of the day tomorrow to capture some wildlife on film." Chyna's reputed hobby as a wildlife photographer was the perfect excuse for Kate to get away from the spying eyes at the ice hotel ... and get those pictures of the penguins she'd promised Gideon.

Crowder nodded at her. "A wise decision. I hope your night is restful as well."

Kate favored him with a fake smile, raised her brows at the others, then turned on her heel and glided off toward her room.

Chapter Seven

Kate woke up feeling more rested than she had in years. Aside from being awakened by a thumping noise in the middle of the night, she'd slept straight through with no dreams that she could remember. *Maybe there is something to sleeping in an ice room*, she thought as she poked her face out from under the heated sleeping bag.

Checking her watch, she was surprised to find it was eight a.m. She never slept that late.

Bounding out of the warm bed into the chilly air, she rummaged through her cosmetics case for the transmitter Gideon had hidden in a makeup compact. Slipping it into the pocket of her thermal pants along with the Tic-Tac's, she grabbed her jacket, gloves, sunglasses, scarf and hat. Throwing the strap of the Nikon camera Gideon had sent over her shoulder, she slipped on her fur boots and made her way out to the lobby.

Crowder was sitting on the ice sofa, sipping a coffee. He stood at her approach.

"Sleep well?"

Kate nodded. "I think I did hear something at one point, but for the most part I was out like a light. This fresh air works wonders."

"You probably heard Mr. Nguyen," Crowder said.

"Nguyen?"

"Yes, he had an attack during the night and we had to rush him out so he could get medical attention." Crowder made a sad face and took a sip from his coffee.

"I see," Kate said. "Well, I do hope he will be okay."

Crowder's eyes drifted down to take in her outfit. "Are you running off somewhere?"

"Yes." Kate indicated the camera slung on her shoulder. "I'd like to try to get some pictures of the penguins ... you wouldn't happen to know where I can find them?"

Crowder shook his head and Fritz, who was hovering nearby piped in. "I hear they nest five miles to the north."

Kate raised her brows. Five miles wasn't very far, in fact it was the perfect distance for what she needed to do. She turned to Crowder. "Might I have use of one of the snowmobiles for the day?"

Crowder pressed his lips together. "We have two new guests arriving today, but as long as you take one of the smaller ones, I think that will be fine." He turned to Fritz. "Show Ms. Hunt which one."

Fritz nodded and Kate jammed the sunglasses onto her face, then followed him out the door.

Outside it wasn't much colder than it was inside. The sun's rays were weak, but warming. Kate followed Fritz around the side of the hotel to where several snowmobiles sat in a row. Without a word, Fritz handed her a key, pointed to a snowmobile and left.

Kate noticed she was in the back of the hotel. An opening led to what she assumed was the kitchen and she couldn't help but peek in. It was empty, save for one man in what looked like an insulated chef's outfit who was carving a turkey. A stainless steel stove sat against the wall next to a series of stainless steel tables, which held an assortment of knives.

There was no fridge, but then again they didn't need one—the low temperature kept everything cold and the snow acted as an icebox as evidenced by the vegetables and meat that were packed in it. They even had those little juice bags that came complete with a straw sitting in rows inside a container carved out of snow.

Turning from the kitchen, Kate straddled the seat of the snowmobile and inserted the key. It started up easily and she glanced at the sun, then at the round compass on the dashboard. North was behind her.

She sat down on the seat, applied pressure to the gas caliper and edged the snowmobile forward. She turned it around slowly, getting used to working the gas. Once satisfied, she goosed it and sped off toward the north.

The arctic air bit into her cheeks as she flew across the glacier, and she wrapped the scarf around the bottom of her face to hide her skin from the chill. The sun glinted off the pristine snow creating an unwelcome glare. Kate squinted at the empty space ahead. There wasn't another person or animal in sight. Glancing back, she noticed the ice hotel was getting smaller and smaller. Not too much longer and she'd be out of sight.

Pressing forward, she felt an immense sense of freedom. Here she was, alone in the wilds of Antarctica ... suddenly she knew why Gideon had seemed so excited. Of course, being out here alone did have its dangers, but she was well trained in survival and it would be easy for her to find her way back. Plus, she needed to get far away from the hotel in order to transmit the data back to Benny.

After fifteen minutes, she came to an inlet with open water. *This must be the five-mile mark where the penguins would be.* She stopped the snowmobile about one hundred feet from the water. No penguins in sight.

But Kate had other, more important business to tend to anyway. She slipped the Tic-Tac camera and compact out of her pocket. Using a special ultra-thin cable about the width of fishing line, she tethered them together and then clicked the button on the compact. A small red light came on, then turned green and Kate sat back on the seat of the snowmobile and scoured the area for penguins while she waited for the transmission to complete.

As she looked around something caught her eye. A flash of light off in the distance—a reflection. Her heart lurched in her chest. Was someone else out here? Watching her? It was impossible. This area of Antarctica was desolate. No one was around for miles except for Crowder, his staff and the rest of the auction goers.

She could have easily been followed from the ice hotel … but who would follow her and why?

Taking the camera out of the bag, she knelt on the snowmobile seat and aimed it in the direction of the reflection, zooming in on the area. Nothing. She moved the camera in a slow arc, zooming in and out, hoping she could catch a glimpse of whoever was out there. *If* anyone was there. After making a full sweep, she put the camera down. She hadn't seen anyone, not even a penguin.

Glancing at the compact, she noticed the light was yellow. Transmission complete. She'd sent Benny the pictures of the auction room, the case the ruby was kept in, and the laser trip wires. His job was to analyze it and come up with a plan for her to disarm the room so she could grab the ruby and run.

They'd already planned her exit strategy and Sal was supposed to meet her at three a.m. with the ski-cycle. She'd need to analyze the plan from Benny, figure out how long it would take, and work backward from there in order to get to the rendezvous point outside her room by three.

Kate figured she had an hour or two before Benny would be able to transmit his information back. Then she'd head back to the ice hotel, plug that info into her laptop and study it. In the meantime, she had some penguins to find.

Sitting back on the seat, she started the snowmobile up and headed further north.

***

It was past noon by the time Kate returned to the ice hotel with half of her tasks completed—she'd received the transmission from Benny, but hadn't found a single penguin.

She felt a twinge of guilt that she'd be disappointing Gideon, but seeking out the penguins *had* provided a great excuse to get away from the hotel to communicate to the ship. Even though the communications would be encoded, it was better if no transmissions came from her room at the hotel ... just in case someone was watching. She didn't want to give them any cause to be suspicious of her.

She parked the snowmobile in its spot and brought the key back into the lobby where Crowder was lurking in his tuxedo-style ski suit.

"Any luck?" he asked as she handed over the key.

"Unfortunately, no. I did not see even one penguin ... no tracks, nothing."

"Well, perhaps tomorrow, then? The auction doesn't start until noon so you have the morning to chase penguins."

"Perhaps." Kate shrugged. *Except I'll be long gone by then.*

"Would you like lunch?" Crowder asked.

Kate's stomach growled and she remembered she'd skipped breakfast. She glanced in the direction of the kitchen.

"We don't have anything too fancy since we have a big dinner planned. Roast duck tonight." Crowder puffed up proudly. "But we do have some sandwiches."

"A sandwich would be adequate," Kate said. "I'm rather tired from all the activity. I'll bring it to my room."

Crowder crooked his finger and a young girl who had been standing inconspicuously by the kitchen came over.

"Turkey or tuna?" Crowder asked Kate.

"Turkey."

The girl nodded and scurried off to the kitchen.

"The other two guests have arrived. I don't think you know them." Crowder's brow furrowed while Kate felt a surge of relief. "They're not collectors, but are assignees of the collector that wants to bid."

"I see." Kate waved a hand dismissively as if the assignees were of no consequence to her. "It's too bad about Mr. Nguyen ... although one less bidder is good for me, I suppose."

Crowder nodded. "And bad for me. But I did get word that Nguyen would be fine."

"Well, that's a relief." The girl appeared beside Kate with a small tray, which held the turkey sandwich and an apple. Kate took the tray, thanked the girl and then turned to go to her room.

"If you need anything else ... anything at all," Crowder said suggestively. "I'll be happy to oblige."

Kate's appetite spoiled as she turned to see Crowder leering at her. She drew herself to her full height and looked down her nose at him, her eyes as cold as steel.

"I assure you I will not be needing a thing," she said, then turned and marched toward her room.

***

Inside her room, Kate locked the door, then put the tray down and dug out her laptop. She sat on the bed with the sandwich beside her and laptop in her lap.

Connecting the compact to the laptop with a special cable, she pulled the file off the compact and munched on her sandwich while a program her father had installed on the laptop decoded it.

Kate studied the information. The pictures hadn't revealed any additional security, so she only had to deal with the laser tripwires and the case the ruby was in. Benny had been able to determine the case was a simple cyber lock and Kate had brought a jamming device, cleverly disguised inside a tampon, so she'd be able to deal with that easily. The rendezvous time was still set for three am outside the west wall of her room. Kate double-checked the coordinates on her cell phone just to be sure.

So, that only left the laser security ... and the giant that guarded the door. Kate wondered if he was there guarding the room all the time. She hadn't seen him anywhere else in the hotel. Did he stand there all night? She'd have to figure out a way to distract him so she could jab him with the sleeping serum. Her stomach twisted as she glanced at her backpack ... she hoped the vial would deliver enough dosage to knock out someone his size.

Turning her attention back to the computer, she studied the map Benny had sent. It was more like a series of dance steps than a map and represented the positions Kate would have to contort her body into in order to dodge the laser beams. Since there was no way to figure out the code, she couldn't risk disarming it—she'd have to depend on her agility to get her to the case and out again. Kate wasn't worried; she'd done it before.

She practiced the steps, getting the feel for each position, memorizing the movements until she felt confident she could repeat them in her sleep.

Once she was satisfied she had everything in order, the information committed to memory and the routine down pat, she deleted any trace of the files and software program from her computer, then snuggled into the sleeping bag for a nap.

***

Kate woke from her nap just before six. Once again, she'd slept like a baby and felt rested and alert ... which was good since she'd be knocking out a giant, stealing the world's largest ruby and making a dangerous getaway in about eight hours.

In the meantime, though, she had to join the rest of them for supper in half an hour.

Kate reluctantly wriggled out of the heated sleeping bag and checked her wig and makeup. The wig had become increasingly itchy and she poked her fingers around inside it trying to scratch her scalp without dislodging the piece. She had to admit, she looked surprisingly good for someone who hadn't showered in two days. *Maybe I don't smell so good though*, she thought, as she dug in her backpack for the perfume vial containing the knockout serum.

Chewing her bottom lip, she sat back down on the bed. She still had no idea how she was going to distract the giant guard. A sexy outfit? A feigned illness? Those were both dangerous plans—what if he didn't fall for them and raised an alarm? It would be much better if she could catch him by surprise, somehow ... but how?

She pushed herself up from the bed. Hopefully, something would come to her, but now it was time for dinner.

Kate slipped out into the hallway, wishing she didn't have to go to dinner. If she didn't show up, it might raise suspicion and she couldn't risk that. Better to suffer through it, and she *did* need to eat.

The hallway spilled her out into the lobby where Crowder stood with his back to her talking with the rest of the guests.

Crowder spun around to face her "How was your afternoon, Ms. Hunt?"

"Fine," Kate said, acting like she was a queen talking to a servant.

"I'd like to introduce you to our new guests." Crowder stepped aside indicating two men who stood a bit away from everyone else. "Jason Smith and Parker Westlake."

Kate's heart lurched. She *knew* Westlake ... or rather he looked familiar. She was sure that wasn't his real name. As she shook hands with him, she searched his face for any signs that he recognized her. For a split-second, she thought she saw something in his eyes, but she might have imagined it as his face became passively indifferent the next time she looked.

"Our new guests haven't seen the items in person yet." Crowder's voice broke into Kate's thoughts. "Shall we all go look at them?"

The crowd murmured its agreement and they started down the hall that led to the secured room. Kate followed, figuring she could use the opportunity to double check the intel she'd already gathered.

The tall guard stood at the door just as he had the night before. This time, Kate noticed a chair that had been carved into the opposite wall. Probably a place for him to rest when no one was around. Kate looked over her shoulder to check the angle. If the guard was seated, he wouldn't be able to see anyone who was approaching from the lobby until they turned the corner. Too bad Kate couldn't think of a way to use that to her advantage.

Crowder went through the same routine as the previous night; punching in the code, turning off the laser system, and then turning on the lights. They piled into the room where Crowder rattled on about each piece for the benefit of the new people. Kate and the others milled around, inspecting the other pieces.

Kate tried to remain aloof just like the real Chyna Hunt would. She stood in front of the ruby, pretending to look at the piece itself, but really studying the case to make sure she could open it.

"'Tis a beauty, no?" Kate turned to Carmen who had snuck up beside her.

"It sure is." Kate looked coolly at the other woman.

"Will you bid on it?" Carmen asked.

Kate shrugged.

"You will get no competition from me," Carmen added. "I only collect jewels I can wear. Like those." She nodded toward the case with the jeweled crown, which Kate noticed had a matching necklace, bracelet and earrings.

"Those sure are nice," Kate said. "But I prefer pearls."

Carmen laughed. "So I hear. It's good we will not compete. Maybe I can get my jewels at a bargain. I hear they were once in the possession of the ancestor of Katherine the Great."

Kate narrowed her eyes at the other woman. "And you don't mind that they were stolen? Where would you wear them?"

Carmen laughed. "Only to the most secretive of functions. But surely, none of us mind acquiring the stolen goods or we would not be here."

Kate nodded. "My grandfather has many such pieces ..."

"Who's ready for supper?" Crowder's announcement saved Kate from having to discuss acquiring stolen treasures any further and the two women headed toward the door where Crowder ushered all the guests into the hallway.

As they headed off toward the dining room, Kate looked back over her shoulder in time to see the guard reactivate the alarm, then slip into the seat carved into the ice wall.

They spread out around the table. Kate tried to keep as much distance between her and Westlake as possible. He didn't seem to be paying any special attention to her at all, so Kate chocked up her earlier impression to nervousness. She'd be glad when everyone went to sleep and she could grab the ruby and get out of there.

Everyone ordered drinks. Kate stuck to a glass of wine, from which she planned to take as few sips as necessary to blend in with everyone else—she didn't need alcohol dulling her senses.

Once again, the meal started with a soup— this time it was lobster bisque. Kate slurped along with the rest of them.

"Isn't this delicious?" Carmen, who had been seated next to Kate, asked.

Kate half turned and nodded. She wanted to discourage conversation as much as possible. Carmen ferried the spoon to her lips and took a dainty sip, then grabbed her scotch on the rocks to wash it down. Kate noticed she was using a small straw—an old trick Kate had used herself to keep from smearing her lipstick.

The straw gave her an idea.

The rest of the dinner was uneventful. She made small talk with a few of the guests but most everyone kept to themselves, which suited Kate just fine.

When the last of the decadent double chocolate cheesecake had been cleared away, Crowder stood up. "Would you all like to join me for drinks in the main room?"

Mrs. Powell who had been overindulging in mimosas tittered an affirmative reply. Mr. White raised his glass full of something amber. "Here. Here."

Carmen swooped up her cocktail and headed toward the door. Simon, Smith and Westlake glanced around the table, but made no move to join Crowder. Kate got the distinct impression that they, like her, were not here for the social aspects.

Kate patted her lips with her napkin and stood up. "I think I'll just grab a juice and go to my room."

"As you wish," Crowder said. "Anyone who wants drinks, head on out to the lobby. And don't forget ... the auction is tomorrow at noon!"

Kate made her way toward the door to the kitchen where she was met by the same girl that had brought her the sandwiches.

"I was wondering if I could have one of those juice boxes to take to my room?" Kate asked. "Apple if you have it."

"Of course." The girl ducked into the kitchen, then came out with the juice and handed it to Kate.

"Thanks." Kate grabbed the juice, checked her watch, then hurried to her room.

Chapter Eight

While everyone else was busy drinking, laughing, and—Kate hoped—falling into a deep slumber, Kate was busy preparing to steal the ruby.

She'd spent the first few hours practicing the steps she'd need to get around the lasers. Then she'd checked and double checked all the equipment and laid out the special black pants and shirt—battery heated, of course—which looked like a normal shirt and pants to the naked eye, but were coated with something that would make her virtually invisible in a dark room.

Finally, with only thirty minutes to go, she crept over to her door and cracked it open, sticking her head out into the hallway, straining to hear if anyone was out and about. Silence.

She crept down to the lobby, the tension in her shoulders relaxing when she found it empty. Even the kitchen was dark and still. Perfect.

Kate ran back to her room and emptied out her backpack, leaving only the laptop and other things she would escape with after making sure there was enough room for the ruby. She removed the jumble of combs and pins that held the wig in place, sighing in relief when she finally pulled the itchy thing from her head.

She smiled, imagining the look on Crowder's face when he found it on top of her bed. Somehow, knowing that *he'd* know he'd been faked-out by an impostor gave her great satisfaction. And it would also clear Chyna Hunt's name in underground circles—according to Max, she hadn't minded lending her name to the cause, but didn't want people thinking she really *was* a thief. Leaving the wig would accomplish that nicely.

She changed into the black outfit and pulled on a black ski mask that covered her entire face with only tiny slits for her eyes. Special battery heated gloves fitted to her fingers would allow her to work effectively without anything thick to impede her fingers, but still keep them warm.

Reaching into the suitcase, she pulled out a box of tampons and selected one that she ripped apart to reveal the frequency jammer for the case the ruby sat in. She shoved it in her pocket along with a pair of high-tech wire cutters she had hidden in the camera case. They looked like regular cutters, but would disrupt the signal from the door wire and return the signal so the system wouldn't be aware the circuit had been broken.

Grabbing the perfume vial, she unscrewed the top, removed the side holding the needle and vial of serum, and placed it carefully on the table.

Finally, she turned to the juice drink that had been sitting on the faux fireplace mantle. It was still very cold, in a slush-like state. Being in an ice hotel did have its advantages when it came to keeping drinks cold, but that didn't matter to Kate, because she wasn't going to drink it.

Ripping the straw off the drink package, she loaded it up with the needle and vial, taking care not to prick herself with the serum—it wouldn't do to knock herself out before she had a chance to get the ruby.

Noting the time, she double-checked she had everything ready and just where she wanted it, then she made her way to the door. Resting her hand on the handle, she took a deep breath and let it out slowly, willing her nerves into a calm state.

She'd have only one chance to get this right. She needed a calm mind and nerves of steel. She couldn't risk screwing up because of shaky hands or a bad decision—not only because it would ruin the chances of recovering the ruby, but also because her life may depend on it. God only knew what Crowder would do to her if he caught her.

***

Kate slipped out into the hall, checking both ways before she crept off toward the lobby. She flattened herself against the wall at the corner where the lobby turned into the hallway to the secured room. Taking another deep breath, she peeked quickly around the corner then drew her head back in a single motion.

The giant was there, sitting in the ice chair with his head angled away from her, looking toward the door to the secured room.

Kate looked at the straw in her hand. She'd only have one chance to hit the giant and she'd better make it count. Taking a deep breath, she lifted the straw to her lips, stepped out into the hallway and aimed.

Kate's heart skipped when the giant rose from his chair and turned to face her. She stood there frozen as he took one step toward her, at the same time his hand flew to his neck. She saw his eyebrows dip together ... and then he crashed to the floor.

Kate's pulse raced as she ran toward him. Was he really out? Did anyone hear him fall? She flattened herself against the wall, straining to hear if anyone was coming, but there was only silence.

She bent down to check the giant. The makeshift dart had hit him in just the right spot in his neck, and she gave a silent prayer of thanks for her childhood education at the hands of her parents and their friends. She'd learned a lot of unusual skills that had come in handy over the years, and shooting darts out of a straw was one of them. He was out like a light, but still breathing.

Taking out the wire cutters, she bent down in front of the door and attached them to the wire, holding her breath and waiting to hear the alarm that would raise the others. No alarm. She pushed the door open and stepped inside.

The room was pitch-black except for the eerie white lights coming from the platforms the ruby and jewelry sat on and the red laser beams that crisscrossed around the room.

Kate went through the steps in her head as she stared at the lights, double-checking that the movements matched with where the lights fell. Satisfied, she stepped forward, raising her right leg over a beam of red light. Then she spun, angling her left hip upward as she raised her leg to the knee, threading her calf, thigh and then entire body in-between two beams of light. Next, she bent at the waist and crawled forward through more beams.

To anyone looking in, it might have looked like some strange kind of dance or an odd game of twister. Except no one looking in would actually be able to see her. The black outfit and stocking mask made her all but invisible. Of course, the sleeping giant in the hallway might give away the fact that things were amiss. Kate picked up the pace. She needed to grab the ruby and get out before someone woke up and found him.

Finally, she got to the case that housed the ruby. Taking out the jamming wand, she applied it to the case. The lights on the wand flickered … then came on strong, indicating it had done its job. Holding her breath, Kate lifted the top— slowly at first, then, when no alarm sounded, she whipped it off, grabbed the ruby and stuffed it in her backpack.

Repeating her strange dance in reverse, she made her way back to the door. Opening it, she looked out into the hall. It was empty except for the guard who lay snoring on the floor.

She slipped into the hall, tiptoed over the guard, and ran for the front door.

Chapter Nine

Outside, there was nothing but silence. Kate had a moment of panic, wondering what she would do if Sal wasn't there with the ski-cycle. But then she rounded the corner and saw him at their meeting spot. She whistled her best imitation of an owl hoot—their designated signal —and Sal gave her the thumbs up, then swung the cycle around to meet her.

She grabbed the puffy down jacket from the back of the bike to keep her warm during the ride and shrugged into it. Swinging one leg over the back of the bike, she settled into the seat, a bubble of triumph rising in her chest. She'd pulled it off! She tapped Sal's arm in a signal to take off and the cycle rushed forward.

Kate was surprised at how quiet the machine was. The snowy landscape was like a blanket dampening any other sounds and Kate marveled at the nighttime beauty of Antarctica as they raced across it. Pulling off her ski mask, and looking upward she realized the stars really were brighter here—just like Gideon had said. She felt a pang of regret that she hadn't been able to get any penguin pictures for him.

Her pulse started to creep back to normal and she relaxed on the back of the ski-cycle, the dark, silent night almost lulling her to sleep.

Thwack!

Kate's nerves snapped to attention. *What was that?*

She felt a rush of air blow past her cheek, then her heart stuttered as she saw something rip through the sleeve of her coat and embed itself in Sal's thumb.

A dart? Why would someone be shooting darts?

Kate thought about the dart with the knock out serum she'd shot into the giant guard and her heart froze. What if *these* darts had something worse on them … something deadly?

She didn't want to find out.

"Someone's shooting at us! Put up the shield!" She tapped Sal on the shoulder and pointed to the dart in his thumb wondering how he could possibly not have noticed.

Sal pressed the button and the back shield rose up, causing the bike to slow. Kate glanced back to see a row of snowmobiles in the distance. Three … no four … and they were gaining.

"Faster, Sal, they're gaining!" She could hear the motors now as whoever was chasing them pushed the vehicles to go faster.

"We're almost there," Sal shouted as Kate watched the black specs grow larger.

Thwack. Thwack.

Darts bounced off the Plexiglass shield and Kate reminded herself to thank Gideon for installing it ... if she ever saw him again.

Kate turned forward, her stomach sinking when she saw the dart in Sal's thumb. "Sal, your thumb! We need to get that dart out!"

Sal waved her off. "Don't worry, it doesn't hurt."

"But it could be poison!" Kate's gut wrenched. What would happen if Sal passed out —or worse—while he was driving? The bike would stop and the bad guys, whoever they were, would catch up to them. Then where would they be?

But Sal only pushed the cycle faster. "It's only a half mile more!"

Kate looked back again, her heart pounding in her chest. They were getting closer and she realized the big flaw in her plan—she didn't have a weapon to defend herself.

"Hold on!" Sal shouted and Kate whipped her head forward in time to see the black ocean approaching. Her gut tightened as it got bigger and bigger—it was coming up at an alarming rate and she wondered if the ski-cycle was built to splash into the ocean at this speed, or if the whole thing would sink. The ocean was frigid and she wouldn't survive in there long, but that death was probably preferable to what would happen if her pursuers caught her.

"Geronimo!" Sal shouted as they approached the edge of the iceberg.

Kate's heart jumped into her throat as the bike sailed off into thin air.

Glancing down at the black, cold waters below, Kate realized the iceberg was only about seven feet off the water—but it felt like seventy, because time had slowed down. Kate felt a sickening sensation, like she'd left her stomach back on the glacier as they shot out into oblivion. She stared at the dark, star-studded sky ahead of her and noticed it was nearly impossible to tell where the sky ended and the water began—it was all just black except for the light of the stars and a few moonbeams that danced off the waves.

And then they were losing altitude. Her stomach apparently caught up to her and then proceeded to crowd into her throat. She heard a click, and the flotation platforms shot out of the side of the cycle.

Maybe she wouldn't die, after all ...

As the ski-cycle headed down toward the water, she risked a glance back at the glacier. The snowmobiles had stopped at the edge—they couldn't follow them into the water. She noticed the men jumping off and aiming something at them just as they disappeared from her line of vision.

She looked down to see how close she was to the water. And that's when she saw them. Penguins. Dozens of them floating on an iceberg.

She pulled the Tic-Tac camera from her pocket just before the ski-cycle splashed into the cold arctic waters. She was determined to get pictures of the penguins for Gideon ... even if it was the last thing she did.

***

Kate climbed up the ladder and heaved herself over the side of the boat, thankful that getting pictures of the penguins wasn't the last thing she ever did.

"Katie!" Her father rushed over, crushing her in a bear hug. "I'm so glad you're okay—we saw you being chased through the binoculars."

Kate wriggled out of her father's grasp.

"Sal got shot ... well, darted! We need a tourniquet, bandages maybe even hot water!" Kate ran over to Sal. "You better lay down." She waved her hand at one of the teak lounge chairs on the deck of the boat.

Teak lounge chairs?

Kate did a quick survey of the deck, noticing it looked more like a pleasure ship than a research vessel. Her parents and several of the *Golden Capers* retirees stood around.

Did they have drinks in their hands?

Kate's brows flew together as she noticed her mother was handing her a martini. She looked over at Sal.

Why was everyone just standing around and not tending to him?

"Sal needs help. Why are you all just standing ar—?"

"This?" Sal cut off her words, holding up his thumb with the dart still sticking out of it. "It's nothing to worry about."

Kate's eyes went wide as he reached over with his other hand and removed the entire thumb, dart and all.

"You have a prosthetic thumb?"

Everyone laughed and Kate felt relief, then anger. Relief that Sal wasn't hurt, anger that everyone was laughing at her.

"Yeah, I lost my thumb back in Berlin when we did the Covsner job." Sal's eyes got a faraway look. "You remember that one, Vic?"

"I sure do," Vic said.

"Yeah, those were the days," Benny added.

"Why darts?" Gertie, one of the *Golden Capers* retirees who had been an expert safe cracker back in the day, held Sal's thumb up in front of her face.

"That's a good question." Kate looked back at the glacier, which was now empty. Who were those men on the snowmobiles?

"They were probably afraid that gunshots might cause the iceberg to break up or start an avalanche," Benny offered.

"Were those Crowder's men chasing you?" Vic asked,

I'm not sure." Kate pursed her lips together. "I never saw that many men at the ice hotel ... but who else could it have been?"

"Well, you're safe now, dear." Carlotta helped Kate wriggle out of the backpack. "Is the ruby inside?"

"Yes." Kate sipped the martini, enjoying the sting in the back of her throat.

"I've been dying to get a look at it." Carlotta pushed a pile of empty drink glasses aside and set the bag on a glass-topped table. "May I?"

"Sure." Kate collapsed into a chair, coming down from the rush of adrenalin and starting to feel a sense of elation and pride that she'd pulled the job off and was on her way back to the museum with the ruby.

She sipped her drink as she watched her mother take the ruby out of the backpack and place it carefully on the table, walking around the table in a circle to look at it from all sides.

Kate's stomach started to sink as she noticed Carlotta's forehead crease slightly. Carlotta bent down level with the table to stare at the ruby, then tilted her head this way and that to see it from all angles. Kate didn't like the way her mother's lips were drawing tighter and tighter together.

Finally, Carlotta looked up at Kate—the look in her eye causing Kate's heart to sink.

"This isn't a real ruby ... it's a fake."

Chapter Ten

"What do you mean it's a fake?" Kate stood in the middle of Gideon's lab, with her fists planted on her hips as she watched him inspect the Millennia Ruby with a magnifying glass refractometer.

He looked at her, his owlishly large green eyes apologetic. "Sorry, but this rock is not an actual gemstone." He held the magnifying glass to the rock and motioned for her to look through it. "See how the bubbles and striations are uniform? How it has curved lines?"

Kate nodded.

"Well, that indicates this is glass. Real gemstones and crystals don't have uniform bubbles or swirls."

Kate stood back, crossing her arms against her chest. "So Max sent me on a wild goose chase, risking my life to steal a big hunk of glass?"

Gideon shook his head. "No. The Millennia Ruby that we had in the museum was real. I verified it myself."

"So what are you saying? Someone stole the real ruby and replaced it with a fake?"

"That's the only logical conclusion."

Kate sighed as she flopped into one of the chairs. Daisy jumped up into her lap, licked her face and then curled up in a ball. Kate stroked the dog's silky ears. "But why would someone do that?"

Gideon shrugged. "Well, either the person that stole it gave a fake to Crowder ... or Crowder had it faked and was trying to pass it off to someone at the auction."

Kate pressed her lips together. "Crowder would have to be really stupid to pass off a fake ruby. It would ruin his reputation, not to mention whoever he sold it to might kill him for it."

"I'm sure he must have the items that get consigned to the auctions inspected by his own people," Gideon said. "Like you say, it is his reputation on the line and he's getting these things from thieves, so surely he would want verification."

"Right, he wouldn't have gotten as far as he did in that business if he didn't take steps to ensure he was selling the real thing."

Gideon's computer made a coughing noise and Kate's brows drew together as she looked over at it.

"There's one other solution." Kate's stomach flip-flopped as she heard Max's velvety smooth baritone come out of the computer. She narrowed her eyes at Gideon ... had Max been listening in all along?

"What's that?" Kate asked, shooting up from the chair and dumping Daisy to the ground in her rush to get over to the computer monitor.

"Someone stole it *after* Crowder verified it, and replaced it with a fake to buy time before anyone realized it had been stolen."

"Who would do that?" she asked, sliding into the chair in front of the computer and angling the monitor to face her. "That seems risky ... I mean, when would they even have the opportunity?."

"Same time you did."

Kate fiddled with the monitor, but the screen wouldn't come on. "You mean at the ice hotel?"

Kate slapped the side of the monitor, trying to get it to respond.

Gideon noticed Kate whacking the monitor and came over to help. "That would be the perfect place. The thief would know it had already been validated by Crowder and no one would suspect a switch until after the auction once the new owner had the ruby verified ... if they even bothered."

"Precisely," Max said. "No one would be looking for the ruby since no one would know it was stolen."

"Jeez, that seems like an awful lot of work and risk," Kate said leaning over the monitor to tug on the cables in back of it. "And if it's true, that means someone at the ice hotel still has it. Once Crowder notices it's missing, he'll search everyone and they'll be caught."

"Actually, they won't," Max said. "You covered for them perfectly. Crowder will think Chyna's imposter stole it and look no further."

Kate's stomach sank, not only had she disappointed Max by bringing back a fake ruby, but she'd made it possible for someone else to get away with the real ruby.

"Boy, that thief is going to be happily surprised when they wake up and find out someone stole the fake ruby," Kate said.

"They'll have a free ride since everyone will be looking for the Chyna Hunt imposter," Gideon added, bending under the table and coming up with the unattached end of the monitor cord.

"Frankly, I think it's a lot of trouble to go through for this particular item. But it makes me want it back even more," Max said. "Kate, this makes your job a little easier since you were at the hotel and you know all the people involved— you simply need to figure out which one of them stole it from a very narrow list of suspects."

Kate exchanged a glance with Gideon—Max made it sound like it was going to be so easy. "Right, of course. Piece of cake."

Kate heard a knock coming from the computer and then the voice of Mercedes LaChance assaulted her ears. "Your appointment is here, Max."

Kate felt a jolt of panic—Max was about to sign off! She grabbed the monitor cable out of Gideon's hand.

"I've got a meeting now, but Kate?" Max paused.

"Yes?" Kate prompted as she shoved the cable end into the monitor.

"I know you'll do a great job."

"Wait!" The cable connected and the monitor surged to life just in time to see a broad chest in a crisp royal blue shirt standing up from the desk. Kate's spirits deflated as she watched the back of Maximilian Forbes walk away from the computer—her first glimpse of her elusive boss and all she saw was a pair of broad shoulders and a lock of curly black hair.

Kate stared at the monitor, now showing Max's empty chair for a split second, then jumped back in her seat as Mercedes' face filled the screen.

"Hi Gideon." Mercedes smiled widely.

"Hi Mercy." Gideon waved at the screen. Kate raised a brow at him and mouthed 'Mercy?' to which Gideon shrugged.

"I'm having a tuna sandwich delivered to the lab for your lunch, Gid." Mercedes trilled as she looked over Kate's shoulder at Gideon. She shifted her gaze to Kate, her eyes turning cold. "Don't forget to turn in your expense report by the end of the week, Diamond."

Then the screen went blank.

***

Kate slumped back in the chair. Not only had she just wasted three days risking her life to steal a fake ruby, now she had to figure out who stole the real one and try to steal it from *them*. And she'd missed a chance to actually see what Max looked like.

"Don't feel so bad, Kate." Gideon perched on the corner of the desk beside her. "At least you got a chance to see Antarctica. How was it by the way?"

"Cold. Snowy. Dangerous," she said, her heart tugging at his crestfallen look. "But it was beautiful just like you said it would be. The stars, the snow, the peacefulness."

Kate remembered the penguins and took the Tic-Tac box from her pocket, tossing it to Gideon. "I did manage to get some pictures of the penguins, although I can't say how good they came out. I took them while flying through the air on your ski-cycle."

Gideon caught the box in mid-air. "So, the ski-cycle worked out for you?"

"Absolutely. It probably saved my life." Kate shivered, thinking about what might have happened if she didn't have the shield to prevent those darts from finding their way into her back.

"I'm glad you came back in one piece." Gideon got up from the desk and walked over to another table, this one cluttered with bottles, Bunsen burners, test tubes and vials. "I don't know if what was in the darts will help you out, but I'm going to analyze it. I don't, however, need this." Gideon held up Sal's thumb.

"Thanks, I'll give it back to him." Kate reached out and took the thumb, started to put it in her pocket, and then hesitated, wondering where the appropriate place to carry someone's prosthetic thumb was. She'd have to do something special for Sal; he'd let her take the thumb with the dart intact so Gideon would have enough of whatever substance was on it to be able to analyze.

"At least you have only a small list of suspects to work with," Gideon said as he sat down in front of a row of bubbling test tubes.

"Right. Small list." Kate tapped her finger on her lips as she thought about the invitees at the ice palace.

Who was most likely to steal the ruby?

Simon had seemed aloof, cagey. It could have been him. And what about Westlake? He'd come late to the party and Kate swore there was something strange about him. Then again, Simon and Westlake were too obvious. But the Powell's would be the least obvious of all of them. Maybe she should start with them, she couldn't think of anyone less obvious ... except ...

Kate snapped her fingers and shot out of the chair. "I think I know who stole the ruby!"

Chapter Eleven

Gideon had work to do at the lab, so Kate headed home for an afternoon of research. She was still tired after her trip to Antarctica and needed a relaxing afternoon followed by a good night's sleep if she wanted to be refreshed and ready to track down the ruby thief.

Sliding her glass of wine onto the coffee table next to her laptop, she snuggled down into her soft, beige microfiber sofa. Kicking her shoes off, she let out a sigh of contentment. Even though she loved going on adventures, there was a lot of truth to the saying 'there's no place like home'.

She closed her eyes for a split-second then popped them back open again. She didn't have time for napping—she had a job to do. Leaning forward, she pressed the button on her laptop to wake it up from sleep mode, then went straight to google and typed 'Jon Nguyen'.

She scrolled through the listings. There were plenty of Jon Nguyens but none that fit the description of the elderly man she'd met at the ice hotel. She felt certain he was the one who stole the ruby. He had a perfect cover, especially if he was faking the illness. Kate had to admit, his act had been very convincing. Still, needing immediate medical attention was a perfect way to make a getaway and, as Kate recalled, the oxygen tank he kept at his side, was the perfect size for storing the Millennia Ruby. All he had to do was break in, like Kate had, steal the ruby, replace it with the fake, go back to his room and fake the medical emergency. Kate did wonder how he got the giant guard out of the way—maybe they were in on it together?

The specifics of how he stole it didn't really matter—finding him did. Kate scrolled through the pages, glancing at each entry and exploring the ones she thought might lead her to the real Nguyen, the level of wine in her glass diminishing with each page.

"Meow!"

Kate's attention was drawn to the window where the gray tiger-striped tomcat she called Archimedes peered in at her with large yellow eyes from his perch on the fire escape. Kate didn't know if the cat was a stray or belonged to one of the neighbors—she hoped the latter as he did have a collar and looked to be well cared for. He'd been coming to Kate's window ever since she moved into the old brick brownstone two years ago. Kate always let him in—she enjoyed the company and her job consisted of too much travel for her to adopt a pet of her own.

Springing up from the couch, she walked over to the row of seven-foot tall windows—one of the features that attracted her to the apartment in the first place, along with the exposed brick, hardwood floors, vintage architecture and Boston suburb address.

She unlatched the window and poked her head out as the cat slipped inside. The view wasn't much. Kate was on the third floor and the window looked down the length of a black metal fire escape that wound its way down the building and to the alley below. Across the alley was another brick building. Beyond that, she could see a tiny section of the Boston skyline, but only if she angled her head just so. She watched her breath come out in a puff of condensation as she strained to see the view—it was late November and the air was getting cold.

"Meow!"

Kate pulled her head in from the window and latched it shut. She looked down at the cat who was weaving his way around her ankles and her heart tugged—she hoped he had a warm place for the winter.

"Hey Archie, want some tuna?"

"Meow!" Archimedes made a beeline for the kitchen and Kate followed, grabbing a can of tuna from the fridge and putting some on a plate, which the cat gobbled down in record time.

Kate returned to the couch and stared at the computer screen. She couldn't seem to find anything in Google on the Jon Nguyen. She double-clicked on the icon to launch the software program Gideon had given her that searched birth records and driver's license databases, typed Nguyen's name in and sat back while the computer did its work.

Archimedes jumped onto her lap and rubbed his face against her chin before curling up in a ball, his tail tucked around his face. Kate stroked the soft fur, her heart flooding with warmth—it felt good to have another warm body near her, even if it was just a stray cat.

Her eyes drifted to a picture in the center of her oak bookshelf. It showed the view from a crisp white stucco building atop a hill, the white gate and walls framing the view of the crystal blue Aegean Sea. This had been the view from her hideaway in Greece where she'd tracked and captured Damien Darkstone. With the help of Ace Mason. Her gut churned just thinking about it—the picture was a painful reminder of one of the best times of her life that had turned sour.

Fighting the tears that pricked the backs of her eyes, she pushed Archimedes aside and marched over to the picture, laying it face down on the shelf. She had no time to think about the past or cry over what might have been. She had a thief to catch.

Kate poured herself another glass of wine before sitting back on the couch. The computer was still chugging away so she leaned back and sipped her wine. Archimedes wiggled his way into her lap again. Kate thought about her trip to the ice hotel, trying to remember any kind of incident or clue that would lead her to the person who stole the ruby. She couldn't think of anything ... but one thing bothered her—*why* would someone go to all that trouble?

Surely, everyone at the hotel had enough money to buy the ruby—they'd have to be wealthy just to make the trip and it was a sure bet Crowder had checked into everyone that had received an invitation. Maybe the person wanted the ruby so badly they didn't want to risk getting outbid? Maybe Crowder had made some bad investments and had faked all the items, planning on taking the money and disappearing?

Or maybe there was something more significant to the ruby than Kate realized. There had to be something else going on, because it didn't make much sense for anyone to risk stealing the ruby like that.

Kate didn't have much time to think about it because just then the computer pinged. It had finished running Nguyen's name through the databases. Kate leaned forward and sighed as she looked at the information on the screen.

"Well, Archimedes," she said to the sleeping cat, "It looks like I'm going to have my work cut out for me. According to the computer, the Jon Nguyen I met at the ice hotel doesn't exist."

Chapter Twelve

The next day, Kate woke up to bright sunshine. She'd slept well. Archimedes had pawed at the window to be let out around ten and she'd obliged and then gone straight to bed, letting her subconscious work on the problem of how she would figure out who Jon Nguyen really was.

Of course, there was the chance that Crowder knew Nguyen's real identity. People often used an assumed name at these underground auctions when they didn't want their name sullied by buying stolen items. Or they sent someone there to bid for them. Crowder would have checked up on each of his guests so he might have known, but she couldn't very well ask him, so she had to come up with another plan.

Luckily, Kate *had* another plan and, thanks to her stint with the FBI, she knew just where to go to execute it.

The best identity forger in the country, Gustav Smirnoff, happened to be located conveniently nearby in downtown Boston and Kate planned on paying him a visit. She dressed in her most FBI-like outfit—a navy trench coat, white button-down shirt and black slacks. Sure, she didn't work for the FBI anymore—even putting on the outfit made her cringe—but Gustav Smirnoff didn't know she didn't work for the FBI and she had a feeling he'd be a lot more willing to answer questions if he thought she still did.

Kate consoled herself that she wasn't exactly *impersonating* an FBI agent. She didn't plan to show a fake badge or announce herself as FBI, but she hoped Smirnoff's memory of her previous business would be enough. And looking the part couldn't hurt.

She shoved her unruly curly hair into a tight bun at the back of her head in order to look more serious, then grabbed her keys and headed out to her Toyota Corolla.

Smirnoff's business was located in the heart of Boston just off Commonwealth Avenue. Parking in the city was problematic, so Kate parked in a public lot and walked.

The leaves had started to fall from the few stately trees that lined the street and Kate listened to them crunch underfoot as she walked, inhaling the heavy smell of diesel that permeated the city. She listened to the sounds of the traffic and watched birds flitter around on the sidewalk grabbing tiny crumbs and seeds as she walked past a beauty salon, Asian take-out, and a pizza place before turning the corner into the alley that housed the nondescript dry cleaners where Smirnoff did business from the back room.

The bell over the door sounded as Kate opened it and she stepped inside the dimly lit shop, closing the door on the warm sun. An elderly woman stood behind the desk.

"I want to see Smirnoff," Kate said in her most official voice.

The woman raised a brow. "You need dry cleaning?"

"No. I have other business."

The woman looked over her shoulder toward the back of the store uncertainly. "He's not in."

Kate pressed her lips together—what if he really wasn't in? Then she remembered a strange phrase Mason had used when they'd come here before—a code phrase.

"I have a fur coat with a ketchup stain."

The woman's eyes went wide and she nodded, then gestured for Kate to go around the desk and follow her out back. Kate followed, resisting the urge to shout "Yes!" and pump her fists in the air. The woman led her through a hallway, down a set of stairs and through two rooms before stopping in front of a door, which she tapped on three times.

"Come in."

The woman opened the door for Kate then turned and left. Kate went in.

The room was dark and smelled of chemicals. Just like she remembered. Smirnoff sat at a table with photos and plastic cases arranged in front of him, a series of machines—Kate assumed for making fake passports and licenses—sat next to him. His brow creased as he recognized her.

"Again?" His voice was gruff with just a touch of Eastern European accent.

Kate wasn't sure if she should feel flattered that he'd remembered—nearly two years had passed since her previous visit.

"Yep." Kate stood with her legs shoulder-width apart, staring him straight in the eye. "I have some questions."

Smirnoff answered by raising his left brow a fraction of an inch and Kate took that to mean she should ask.

"Does the name Jon Nguyen mean anything to you?"

Smirnoff's breath hitched, his eyes widening. "That's very bad business, very bad."

Kate narrowed her eyes. "But you know the name? You made the identity for him?"

Smirnoff slapped his palm on the table and pushed himself up out of the chair, his six-foot-ten frame looming over Kate, his four-foot wide shoulders blocking the light from the lone bulb that hung from the ceiling behind him. "You people said I'd be protected ... that you wouldn't hurt my business. How many times must I answer?"

Kate hoped he couldn't hear her heart thudding against her chest. She knew he must have been talking about when they'd come before. Mason had assured him they wouldn't let anyone know he'd given them up and they'd make sure the cops didn't shut him down.

She drew herself up to her full height, stepped forward, her face inches from his face ... well, his chest, actually. She hoped her assumed FBI employment and fake confidence was scaring him because he sure as heck was scaring her.

"Who did you make the Nguyen identity for? We won't give you away." Kate crossed her fingers behind her back. The FBI wouldn't, would they?

Smirnoff puffed out his cheeks, the smell of stale cigarettes and egg salad wafted past Kate making her nose wrinkle. He ran his hands through the curly ginger colored hair on top of his head.

"I tell you, I don't know the man's name. I made him an excellent disguise. He was a young man when he started, and I made him old," Smirnoff said proudly.

"But you don't know his name?"

Smirnoff snorted. "In this business, you don't ask for names."

Kate wasn't about to give up. "What do you know about him? Where does he live? Can you describe him?"

Smirnoff narrowed his eyes at her. "Well, I do have the picture."

"Picture? Let me see it." Kate held her hand out and waited while Smirnoff pulled a squeaky drawer out from an old metal file cabinet. He thumbed through to a folder, opened it and pulled out a photo, which he handed to Kate.

Kate stared at it. She didn't recognize him, but at least she had something concrete to go on.

"Thanks." She turned and walked to the door.

"It's the same photo I gave to the other guy yesterday," Smirnoff called after her.

Kate froze in her tracks, her hand on the knob. She turned back around slowly, her eyebrows jamming together in confusion. "Other guy?"

"Your partner." Smirnoff waved his hand in the air. "Are you people stupid? Typical government ... one side doesn't know what the other is doing."

"Oh right. My partner. Yep. He was here yesterday?" Kate asked.

Smirnoff nodded, an exasperated look on his face.

Well, it's good that now we both have a copy." Kate turned back around, opened the door and ran for her car.

Chapter Thirteen

Kate gnawed on her bottom lip as she maneuvered her car through the congested Boston traffic.

Partner?

Was Smirnoff talking about Mason? He must have been. Ace Mason was the only person Kate had ever gone to see Smirnoff with. But why would the FBI detective be interested in Jon Nguyen?

Surely, the FBI couldn't be on the trail of the stolen ruby this fast—there was no way they could possibly know about what happened at the ice hotel. Kate felt a sinking sensation in the pit of her stomach. Was she was losing her touch and the FBI was catching up to her on the trail of the ruby thief, *or* was something else going on that she didn't know about?

Either way she was determined to beat them and recover the ruby first ... she *had* to show Max, the FBI *and* Ace Mason that she was as good ... no, better ... than they were.

She whipped her car into the underground garage at the *Ritzholdt Museum*, pulled into her assigned parking spot and jumped out making a beeline for Gideon's lab.

Gideon was sitting in the middle of the lab, hunched over a beaker full of glowing purple liquid. Kate approached with caution.

"Knock, knock." She tapped on the corner of one of the tables. Daisy raised her head and let out an unenthusiastic woof.

Gideon held his hand up and muttered something that sounded like, "Just a minute."

Kate took a seat and stared at the photo. Smirnoff had done a good job with the disguise. She never would have guessed the guy in the photo was the old man she'd met at the ice hotel, or that the old man had even been wearing a disguise. Finally, she heard the squeak of Gideon's chair as he turned around to face her.

"Sorry, I had to make sure I timed the additions of the ingredients precisely in order for the potion to come out right," He said.

"Potion?" Kate stared at the purple liquid. "What's it do?"

"Oh, it's just a test." Gideon waved dismissively in the direction of the potion. "What brings you here?"

Kate tore her eyes from the glowing beaker, and held the picture out. "I need you to run this through the system and come up with a name."

Gideon took the photo. "Does he have something to do with the ruby?"

"I think so." Kate told him how she had visited Smirnoff after her search for Nguyen came up empty. "Apparently, the FBI was there looking for this guy, too."

Gideon turned from the scanner where he was scanning the photo. "Really? Why would they be there?"

"That's what I was wondering. You don't think they know about the ruby heist at the ice hotel, do you?"

Gideon laughed. "No way. I don't see how they could possibly know it was even stolen from there." His face twisted into a scowl. "Unless they have someone on the inside here."

Kate's heart pinched, she leaned toward him, lowering her voice even though no one else was in the lab. "Do you think someone here could be spying for them? Who?" Kate asked, her thoughts immediately turning to Mercedes LaChance.

"Well, we *are* supposed to be sharing this information with them. We're working together on this," Gideon pointed out.

Kate sighed. It was true, she'd forgotten the FBI was *supposed* to be tracking down the ruby and Kate was actually the one who was working on it under the radar. "But still, it seems like awfully fast work for them to have visited him *yesterday*," Kate said.

"True. We barely found out about it ourselves yesterday." Gideon made a face. "And we both know how slow they are to react to information."

Kate felt a tingle of premonition dance up her spine. "I can't help but feel there's more to this than meets the eye."

Gideon moved over to his computer and tapped on the keyboard. "I'll put a call into Max to see if he's heard anything more about the ice hotel incident."

Kate's heartbeat picked up at the mention of Max's name and she leaped up out of her chair. "We should go up there right now."

Gideon looked up at her. "He's in Belgium."

"Oh." Kate deflated back into her seat.

"I'm texting him right now. He'll call when he can," Gideon said.

"Meanwhile, we just sit and wait for your program?" Kate wasn't very good at sitting and waiting. "How long does it take?"

Gideon shrugged. "Depends on how far it has to look. We might get lucky and it will find a match early or it could take hours."

Kate tapped her fingernail on the table. *Hours?* She didn't know if she could wait hours.

"Maybe I should go to my office and finish up some paperwork." She pushed herself up from the chair, and started toward the door just as it whooshed open, revealing Mercedes LaChance on the other side. The two women sized each other up for a few uncomfortable seconds.

Kate narrowed her eyes at Mercedes. "Have you been talking to the FBI?"

"Oh, you mean that hunky Ace Mason?" Mercedes plastered a look of wide-eyed innocence on her face.

Kate's stomach twinged with something that felt an awful lot like jealousy. No, it couldn't be jealousy ... probably just the bean burrito she'd grabbed before she went to Smirnoff's.

"I am the museum liaison, so I talk to him a lot. But not recently." Mercedes returned her narrow-eyed glare. "They're on our side, you know."

"Right, I know that," Kate said. "But you didn't talk to them yesterday or tell them about the ruby?"

"You mean that you stole a fake?" Mercedes slid her gaze over to the big red crystal that sat in the middle of the table.

Kate flushed with anger—the small brunette sure did have a way of getting to her.

Mercedes looked back to Kate, her lips curled in a smile, her eyes warmed, and for a split second, Kate thought the warmth might be genuine.

"You don't need to get touchy about it." Mercedes laughed lightly and touched Kate on the arm in an almost friendly gesture. "There's no way you could have known. And, no, I haven't told the FBI yet." She turned a quizzical eye to Gideon. "Should I hold off on telling them?"

Gideon shrugged and looked at Kate.

"I guess not, I mean we are supposed to be working with them." Kate ground her teeth together. She *had* to share the information with them but she couldn't shake the feeling that she was going to do all the work and the FBI would swoop in at the last minute and take all the credit.

"Were you going somewhere?" Mercedes bent down to pet Daisy, who, Kate noticed grudgingly, had trotted over to greet her.

Kate glared at the dog. *Traitor.* Then she looked back over at Mercedes who was staring up at her with her doe-brown eyes.

"I was just goin—"

Ding!

"It found something." Gideon bent over the computer, tapping on the keyboard.

Kate rushed to his side, elbowing Mercedes out of the way to get closer to the computer whose screen showed the picture Kate had given Gideon side by side with a license. The man in the license was an exact match. Caleb Summers.

"Caleb Summers," Kate said. "Does that name ring a bell?"

"No." Gideon and Mercedes replied in unison.

Kate made a face. "Let's look through the database of gem thieves and con men. We need to find out just who he is and why he stole the ruby and, more importantly, where we can go to get it back."

Gideon, Kate and, much to Kate's dismay, Mercedes, spent the next hour huddled over the computer. Daisy lay quietly on the floor at their feet. They searched every database and case file for the name Caleb Summers but came up empty.

"I don't get it." Kate scrubbed her fingers through her hair. "How could an unknown pull off a heist like that? He doesn't seem to have any experience or knowledge ... unless he's been very good at keeping his activities hidden."

"Maybe someone hired him," Mercedes said.

Gideon's face lit up. "Of course! Why didn't we think of that before?"

Yeah, why didn't we? Kate wondered as she watched Mercedes fold her arms over her chest with a satisfied smirk.

"I'll check his financials. If someone hired him, he might have had some unusual activity in his bank account," Gideon said as he tapped away on the computer.

Kate slid over to one of the other computers and started her own search into the background of Caleb Summers.

"I can't find anything unusual about him," Kate said about twenty minutes later. "He's just a struggling actor."

"Struggling?" Gideon's forehead pleated as he stared at his computer.

"That's what it says here." Kate pointed to her monitor.

"Oh, really?" Gideon pointed to his own monitor. "Then why does he have a hundred and fifty thousand dollars in his bank account?"

Chapter Fourteen

The money that appeared in Caleb Summers' bank account had been a cash deposit. There was no way for Gideon to trace it, so Kate decided to go straight to the horse's mouth. He lived in one of the less affluent sections of Boston, his twelve story high-rise apartment building loomed over Kate as she weaved her way around a child's plastic big-wheel that had been left carelessly in the walkway.

The main door to the building was propped open with a brick so Kate didn't need to wait to be buzzed in, which was fine with her. Somehow, she felt like she'd have a better chance of actually talking to Summers if he didn't have advance notice of her visit.

The elevator was broken, so she walked up to the fifth floor. The stairway was dirty, the air heavy with the spicy aroma of dozens of tenants' meals, the walls dotted with spurts of amateur graffiti. Kate was glad she brought her gun and a bottle of hand sanitizer.

She emerged on the fifth floor and stopped to suck in some air, promised herself that she'd spend more time at the gym, then proceeded down the threadbare carpeting to apartment 512.

Kate knocked and then cocked her ear toward the door to listen for movement inside. She didn't hear any, so she knocked louder.

"Mr. Summers?" She yelled through the door.

No answer.

She rapped her knuckles as hard as she could, but still no sounds from inside and no one came to the door. Kate's stomach sank—it appeared as if Caleb Summers wasn't home, but she wasn't one to waste a trip and she figured she might still find some answers inside his apartment.

Kate glanced at the hallway on either side of her. It was empty, though surely someone must have heard her knocking and yelling—the walls were thin and she could hear muffled sounds of children crying and adults yelling. But no one came out to see why she was knocking so loudly, which was good. Kate didn't need nosey neighbors interrupting her.

She pulled her leather lock-pick case out of her coat pocket and zipped it open. She bent down to inspect the type of lock and select a tool from the kit. Pulling off her leather glove so she could feel the tool more easily, she inserted the pick into the keyhole and worked it back and forth, her heart jolting when one of the apartment doors on the other side of the hall was ripped open.

Kate palmed the lock pick and stood back as if she was waiting for someone to answer the door. A short, dark-haired woman pulled a toddler down the hallway.

"I don't think he's home," she said as she brushed past Kate.

"Oh, really?"

"He said something about a trip," She called over her shoulder. "I've been taking in his newspaper."

"Okay, thanks," Kate called out as the woman disappeared into the stairwell.

A trip?

That could make it difficult to track him down. But it would give her more time to search his apartment. Kate put the pick back in, jiggled it around until she felt the satisfying click of the lock releasing, then opened the door and slipped in.

Summers' apartment was sparse, decorated with second-hand furniture and crates, plus one whopping sixty-inch big screen TV. Exactly what you might expect from a struggling actor who hadn't had time to spend the extra hundred grand in his bank account yet.

Kate started in the kitchen, not really sure what she was looking for, but hopeful she'd know it when she saw it. She put the glove she'd removed in the hallway back on before touching anything. She probably didn't have to worry about leaving prints, but she'd learned in the FBI that one could never be too careful.

The sink was full of food-encrusted dishes. From the looks of things, they'd been there a few days. Probably not too unusual for a bachelor though, and the neighbor did say he was on vacation. The fridge held a half gallon of sour milk, a loaf of bread, ketchup and peanut butter. Not much different from Kate's own fridge.

The cabinets didn't yield any results so she moved into the bedroom. She looked under the bed, in between the mattress and box spring and then started on the bureau with one ear cocked toward the living room, in case Caleb came home. She wasn't sure what she'd do if he did, but it would be good to have extra warning ... if she could even hear him coming in over the sound of her heart pounding in her chest.

She opened the last bureau drawer and her heartbeat kicked into overdrive. The gray wig, makeup and other fittings Caleb had used to transform himself into Jon Nguyen sat on top of a stack of white t-shirts.

So, it was true, someone *had* hired him to impersonate Nguyen and steal the ruby. Did Summers still have it? Was it somewhere here in his apartment? Kate felt a rush of adrenalin and she kicked her search into high gear.

Two hours later, she'd searched the whole apartment and no ruby was to be found. Now she needed to find Caleb Summers more than ever ... but if he'd gone on vacation like the neighbor said, he could be anywhere. And he might not be planning on coming back.

Kate pressed her lips together as she made a final sweep of the table Caleb was apparently using as a makeshift desk in the living room.

If he went somewhere, why hadn't he taken any money out of the bank?

Kate flipped through the calendar that lay on the desk. It was filled with times and dates, all with the designation "Actors Studio." Apparently, Summers spent a lot of time there—he probably had friends that could tell Kate something. But the rest of the calendar was disappointing. There were no appointments out of the ordinary and nothing to indicate a clandestine meeting with whoever hired him to play the part of Jon Nguyen.

A pile of Actors Studio pamphlets, which included the phone number, address and a schedule of shows, lay on the desk. Kate took one last look around the apartment, then swiped a pamphlet and headed out the door.

***

The Actors Studio was on Tremont Street so Kate hopped in her Toyota and made her way toward Boston's South end. She lucked out and got a parking spot across the street from the old brick building.

She jumped out of the car and scooted across four lanes of traffic, marveling at the fancy carved cement work next to the two-story tall rounded window above the Actors Studio doorway as she stepped onto the brick sidewalk. The attention to detail in the centuries-old buildings of Boston never ceased to amaze her—it was one of the things that made the city so unique.

Grasping the large brass door handle, she swung one side of the oversized oak double door open and walked into a cavernous lobby. She stepped onto the aged hardwood floors polished to perfection and looked around at the old brick walls. Inside there were several cathedral arched doors, which had been retrofitted with glass doors in-between the arches. One of them had "Actors Studio" in old-fashioned gold lettering on the front and she headed in that direction.

"Hello there." Kate was greeted by a tall thin blond man wrapping a long fuzzy fuchsia scarf around his neck and then holding his arms out, the ends of the scarf wound around them. "You like?"

Kate tilted her head. "It's you."

The man smiled. "Thanks. Can I help you?"

"I'm looking for Caleb Summers," Kate said.

"Yes. Caleb." The man screwed up his face and tapped his index finger on his pursed lips. "I don't think I've seen Caleb for a while. Let me get Amanda."

He floated off toward a doorway, ducked his head in and yelled "Mandy!"

Seconds later, a mime appeared in the door. She looked at both of them with an exaggerated quizzical look and fuchsia-scarf said. "She was asking about Caleb."

The mime's eyebrows shot up and she made those annoying motions with her hands like she was trying to get out of a box.

Kate shot a look at fuchsia-scarf. She hoped she wouldn't have to receive all her answers from Mandy in mime.

"I'm his cousin visiting from out of town and I was wondering if you know where he is?" Kate said to the mime.

She stopped with the hand motions and puffed out her cheeks. "No. It's the strangest thing. He was supposed to be here last night for rehearsal, but he never showed. Come to think of it, he hasn't been here all week."

"Is he usually?" Kate asked.

"Yes." Amanda's face wrinkled with concern. "I hope nothing's wrong with him ... did he know you were coming?"

"What?" Kate's brow creased at the question. "Oh, no. It's kind of a spur of the moment visit. Did he mention anything ... like a vacation, or anything he had going on?"

"No" Mandy looked at fuchsia-scarf. "Did he say anything to you, Darrel?"

Darrell shook his head. "No. You must be here with Uncle Roger."

"Uncle Roger?" Kate tilted her head at Darrell.

"Yeah. Isn't he your uncle too?"

"Oh, yes, of course," Kate said. "What about him?"

"He came to take Caleb to lunch last week and Caleb sure seemed nervous. It was almost like he was afraid of him or something."

"Uncle Roger can be a little intimidating," Kate said. "Well, I guess I'll be going, then." She turned toward the door.

"Do you want me to tell Caleb you were looking for him?" Mandy yelled after her.

"Sure," Kate tossed over her shoulder as she pulled the door open. "Tell him his cousin, Ruby, was here."

Chapter Fifteen

Kate's brow creased with worry as she balanced the pizza in her right hand while pressing the elevator button for Gideon's lab. There was something strange about this ruby heist ... things weren't adding up. She hoped Gideon could help shed some light on things, which was why she was bringing him pizza for supper.

The smell of tomato, basil and baked dough made her stomach grumble as Kate jabbed the button repeatedly trying to make the elevator go faster. She'd forgotten to eat lunch and had spent the whole afternoon searching Caleb Summers' place and then trying to track him down at the Actors Studio.

Finally, the elevator dumped her out in the basement and she keyed in the code for the lab door, which whooshed open to reveal Gideon bent over his lab table as usual.

"Soups on!" Kate said as she laid the pizza box down on the table and ripped the lid open. Thankfully, Gideon had the foresight to put some paper plates and napkins on the table.

Kate liberated a slice of pizza from the box and bit in.

"Thanks for picking this up." Gideon joined her at the table, picking out his own slice of pizza.

Kate simply nodded and wiped a string of cheese from her chin, her mouth too full of pizza to speak.

"Did you talk to Caleb Summers?" Gideon asked.

Kate plucked a napkin from the table and wiped the grease from her mouth. "No. I couldn't find him. He seems to have disappeared."

Gideon nodded as he swallowed a bite. "Not surprising ... if he stole the ruby then he'd want to lay low."

"Oh, he stole it all right." Kate leaned over the box and picked out another piece—one with lots of pepperoni. "I found the disguise in his apartment."

"You did?"

"Uh huh."

"Well, that solves one mystery," Gideon said.

"But brings up a few more." Kate slid into one of the lab chairs and folded her pizza in half, then shoved a big section in her mouth.

"Like what?"

"Like where he is. Why he stole the ruby ... and what he did with it," Kate said. "I searched his entire apartment and it wasn't there."

Gideon shrugged. "He probably already handed it over to whoever he was stealing it for."

"Yeah ... probably Uncle Roger."

"Uncle Roger?"

"At the Actors Studio, they said that Caleb's Uncle Roger had come last week and Caleb seemed nervous about him." Kate put her pizza crust down on the plate and wiped her hands. "I wonder if that's who he stole it for."

"Maybe, but how do we find out who Uncle Roger is?" Gideon asked.

Daisy had come over and was whimpering at Kate's feet for a handout. She broke a tiny piece off the pizza crust and fed it to the dog while she thought about that.

"Do they have traffic cameras on Tremont Street?" she asked.

Gideon shrugged as he chewed.

"If they do, we might be able to see this Uncle Roger on the video ... if we can tap into it." Kate raised her brows at Gideon.

"I'll see what I can do." He finished off his piece of pizza. "In the meantime, I found out what was in the darts they were shooting at you."

"Oh really? What was it, some sort of exotic poison that makes you die in agony?" Kate shivered just thinking about it.

"No. It was just a simple tranquilizer. Not even enough to kill you."

Kate's brows mashed together. "Really? That seems strange because they sure seemed like they were out to stop us."

"Stop you ... but not kill you," Gideon said.

The computer on the next table blared forth with an old-fashioned telephone sound.

"Someone's calling on Skype." Gideon got up and ran over to it. "It's Max."

Kate's eyes widened and she ran over to stand beside Gideon. She really wanted to see Max in person, but catching a glimpse of him on the computer screen was better than nothing.

"Hi Max," Gideon said.

"Hello Gideon ... and Kate, I'm glad to see you there, too." Max's voice flowed out of the computer smooth as a river of chocolate. But where was the video? Kate stared at the screen but all she could see was ceiling tiles.

"Max, I think something's wrong with your camera, all I see is the ceiling," Kate said.

"Yeah, this stupid thing ... I can never aim it right," Max said and Kate watched the camera move in dizzying arcs as Max tried to adjust it. "Anyway, I have some important information about the Millennia Ruby case that I wanted to tell both of you."

That had Kate's full attention.

"Yes?" she prompted.

"According to my sources, Crowder wasn't in on the ruby switch. And he was quite surprised when he found his guard passed out the next morning." Max laughed. "Geez Kate, what did you give that guy? I heard he was pretty big. You must have dosed him up with something pretty hard."

Kate glanced at Gideon. "I did give him a double dose of Gideon's knock out serum. I hope he's okay ..."

"He's fine. Well, except he fell on his hand, which was exposed to the snow for a long time and he lost his pinkie to frostbite," Max said. "I hear he's pretty mad at Chyna Hunt ... or her impostor."

"So they know that wasn't really Chyna, then?" Kate asked.

"Yep," Max said as his camera focused on a yellow post it note on his desk. "Is the camera angle better?"

"I hope there's no way for them to find out it was Kate." Gideon's brows dipped together. "I wouldn't want her to be in danger. And the camera looks like it's pointing at your desk."

"Oh don't worry," Max said. "They won't find out it was Kate ... but she still might be in danger." The camera jerked back up to the ceiling again. "Better?"

"It's pointing to the ceiling again. What do you mean I might still be in danger?" Kate glanced uneasily at Gideon.

"Crowder didn't know the ruby was stolen until the next morning, which means he's not the one who was chasing you," Max said.

Kate felt a tingle of unease in her stomach. "So then, who *was* chasing me?"

"I don't know who ... or why." Max's voice turned grim. "There's a lot here that doesn't make sense. Why is someone going to so much trouble over the ruby crystal? I smell trouble and I'm thinking it might be best if we just left recovering the ruby to the FBI."

Kate felt as if she'd been punched in the gut. "You mean you want me to stop investigating?"

"It's not that you're not doing a good job, Kate," Max said. "You've done great, but I don't want to put you in danger. I wouldn't be able to forgive myself if you got hurt."

Kate's heart melted a little at Max's concern but she *couldn't* give up the hunt for the Millennia Ruby. For one thing, Kate Diamond wasn't a quitter, and for another she had to prove to everyone—even herself—that she could get the job done.

"I appreciate your concern, but once I start a job, I like to finish it. So I'll have to refuse your invitation to drop the investigation," Kate said stiffly.

Max sighed. "I figured you'd say that. I guess your persistence is one of the reasons I hired you so I won't force the issue. But I *do* want you to be extra careful, and if things get too dangerous, please back off."

"Okay," Kate agreed.

"And Gideon," Max said. "Make sure you give Kate whatever she needs."

The camera swiveled zooming in on Max's tie.

"Of course," Gideon answered. "The camera's on your tie ... move it up just a hair."

"All right then," Max said. "Let's keep each other informed."

"Right," Kate and Gideon said at the same time. Kate held her breath as the camera panned up from Max's tie. She saw his neck, a square-jawed chin with a bit of sexy stubble ... and then the screen went blank as he signed off.

"Dammit!" Kate banged her fist on her thigh.

"I know, I hate to think you might be in trouble." Gideon turned concerned eyes on her. "You should just give up on the ruby."

"What? Oh, that. That's not what I was upset about. I thought I was finally going to get to see what Max looked like." Kate touched Gideon's arm. "I appreciate your concern, but I'm not going to get hurt. Don't forget I was a trained FBI agent. And I am *not* giving up on finding the ruby."

Kate smiled at Gideon, ignoring the niggling of doubt that was spreading in her chest. Max was right, there were some oddities about the case that were disconcerting, but she could handle it. Besides, finding the ruby *before* the FBI did would be worth any danger she would put herself in and she couldn't wait to see the look on Ace Mason's face when *she* was the one to bring the ruby back.

Chapter Sixteen

Kate didn't have to wait long to see the look on Ace Mason's face. Unfortunately, she wasn't holding the ruby under his nose when she next saw him. In fact, she was at a distinct disadvantage—disheveled, un-showered and with no makeup—since the FBI had practically broken down her door first thing the next morning and demanded her presence downtown.

They were even kind enough to insist on following her car there, just to make sure she didn't get lost.

Kate simmered with anger as she sat in the interrogation room. A dull beige room, it held only a plain metal table and four uncomfortable metal chairs. She'd sat at that table many times —except all the other times she'd been on the opposite side. Somehow, the room didn't have the same appeal when *she* was the one about to be interrogated.

She glanced at the two-way mirror that made up the entire east wall and wondered who was on the other side. Probably someone she knew.

She smiled and waved as if she didn't have a care in the world. Which she didn't, since she wasn't guilty of anything.

The door swung open and Kate looked over, her heart twisting when she saw none other than Ace Mason step through. He was dressed casually. A gray thermal shirt with three buttons down the front clung to his muscular chest in a way that should have been against FBI dress code. His muscular thighs filled out the faded jeans as he walked on thick steel-toed work boots to the opposite side of the table from Kate.

He pulled out a chair and turned it around, then straddled it leaning his forearms on the back of the chair as he faced her.

"Kate, you look ... good." His voice was tinged with sarcasm and his gray eyes sparkled with mischief as he took in her appearance. Kate felt her cheeks grow warm. She silently cursed the FBI for pulling her in first thing in the morning without even letting her brush her hair.

"Just what is this about?" she asked in the haughtiest tone she could muster.

"What do you know about Caleb Summers?" Ace's gray eyes drilled into hers and she fought to keep from looking away.

"Who? I don't think I recognize the name."

"Come on, Kate. We know you know him." Ace kept staring and Kate squirmed in her seat, determined to hold his gaze so as not to end up the loser in the strange staring contest they were having.

"I swear … I've never met him." It wasn't exactly a lie since she'd never met him … at least not as Caleb Summers.

Ace sighed and stood. Kate felt a moment of triumph when his eyes left hers but that was short-lived. He was standing now, forcing her to look up at him, which, Kate realized, gave him a psychological advantage.

"Okay, I can see you're going to make me do this the hard way." Ace rubbed his hand through his short-cropped dark hair as he paced around on the other side of the table. Did Kate see tinges of gray at the temples? She certainly hoped so— the thought of Ace Mason going gray with stress and worry was somehow satisfying to her … even if the gray did make him look even more appealing.

Suddenly he stopped and pivoted to look at her. "I'll give you one more chance, Kate. Tell me what you know or I'll have to hold you as our prime suspect in his murder."

Murder? Kate struggled to remain calm. *Was he saying Caleb Summers was dead?* Kate felt deflated—Summers was her only lead in the theft of the ruby.

"Oh come on, Ace. You know I didn't kill anyone."

"Do I?" Ace asked. "We know very little about what you're involved in since you left the bureau."

"And anyway, you certainly can't have any evidence because I didn't do it," Kate said realizing he must have been bluffing.

"Oh no?" Ace planted his palms on the table and leaned across it, his face heart-thumpingly close to Kate's. "We have witnesses that say you were asking around about him. The pamphlet to his Actors Studio was found in your purse ... and if *that's* not enough, we lifted one of your fingerprints from his doorknob."

Kate's breath caught in her throat. *Dammit!*

Ace smiled triumphantly at her reaction and straightened. "So, you *do* know him."

Kate shook her head. "I never met him. His name came up as a lead in the Millennia Ruby case."

Kate hated to give away any of her leads that might give the FBI an advantage on finding the ruby even though she was supposed to be working together with them. But they obviously already knew about Summers, which Kate found suspicious.

Ace's left eyebrow lifted. "What were you doing at his apartment, then?"

"I went to talk to him, but he wasn't home." Kate's mind raced—how had they found a fingerprint, she was sure she'd worn her gloves. Then she remembered the neighbor interrupting her as she picked the lock. She'd probably forgotten to wipe the doorknob. But the fingerprint on the outside of the knob wouldn't place her inside the apartment.

"And you broke in," Ace persisted.

Kate shifted uncomfortably in her chair under his unwavering gaze. She wasn't very good at lying.

"I didn't find anything," she said in a small voice.

Ace came around to Kate's side of the table and leaned his well-formed butt on the edge. "Tell me why you are so interested in Summers."

Kate narrowed her eyes at Ace. "Why are *you* so interested?"

Kate saw Ace's eyes grow soft and her heart crunched. He leaned toward her, tucking a stray wisp of hair behind her ear and causing her pulse to take off like a horse in the Kentucky Derby. "Kate, there's more going on here than I think you are aware of. Messing in this could be dangerous."

Kate frowned at him.

What was he talking about?

"How did he die?" Kate asked.

"He was found floating in the Charles River."

"Murdered?"

Ace shrugged. But of course they thought it was murder, why else would the FBI be interested? And since they seemed to know so much about it, Kate decided it was probably in her best interest to tell him what she knew—he'd find out soon enough from Mercedes since they were supposed to be sharing their information.

"We have reason to believe that he used a disguise to steal the Millennia Ruby from the person who stole it from the museum," she said.

"And ..." Ace prompted.

"That's it. That's all I know," Kate said "Okay, well, I'm pretty sure it *was* him because I found the disguise in his apartment."

"Why do you think he would do that?"

"I guess someone paid him ... we found a large deposit in his bank account."

Ace nodded. "We did too. But don't you think that's a little excessive for the ruby?"

"Well, now that you mention it, I do." Kate studied Ace. "You know something more about the case, don't you?"

Ace put his hand over Kate's and she looked down at their two hands as hers started to tingle annoyingly underneath his. "I know that you should be careful. You may be into things that are way over your head."

Kate snapped her head back up to look at him.

Did he just say "over her head"?

For a minute there, Kate had been starting to warm to him again, but now she realized he was still a condescending jerk. Clearly, he thought she couldn't handle getting the ruby back and whatever else was going on with the case.

Well, if Detective Ace Mason hoped his warnings were going to get her to stop investigating, he could think again—she was more determined than ever to retrieve the ruby.

Kate jerked her hand out from under his, and pushed herself up out of the chair, her eyes flashing with fury. "This interview is over. I have nothing more to say, so if you want to keep me here, you're going to have to arrest me."

Chapter Seventeen

The FBI didn't have anything to hold Kate on, so they had to let her go. After running home and grabbing a quick shower, she headed over to the museum and straight to Gideon with her suspicions of the *real* reason the FBI pulled her in.

"I knew it!" Kate said as Gideon pulled the tracking device off the underside of her car. "That's the oldest trick in the book. Did Ace Mason think I would fall for that?"

"Do you really think they pulled you in just so they could put this on your car? They could probably do it while it was parked on the street at any time," Gideon pointed out.

"He did press me for information," Kate said. "And tried to get me to back off."

"Why would he want you to back off?"

Kate shrugged. "He said something about me being in over my head."

Gideon's brows shot up. "I bet that went over well."

"Now I'm more determined than ever to get to the ruby before they do," Kate said, then at Gideon's quizzical look she added, "I mean it's most important the museum gets the ruby back no matter what ... but I just want it to be *me* that gets it."

"I understand. You don't want Ace Mason to beat you out."

Kate's gut clenched at the mention of the detective's name. "It's not *just* that ..."

Gideon held the tracking device up in his hand. "So you want me to destroy this so he can't follow you around and steal all your leads?"

Kate held out her hand, a smile tugging at the corner of her lips. "No, I have a better idea. If Ace Mason thinks he's going to put a tracking device in my car so he can get me to do all the legwork, he's going to be in for a little surprise."

Gideon raised a brow as he dropped the tiny device into Kate's hand, but she didn't elaborate on her plan.

"So, now that your lead is dead, what do you plan to do next?" Gideon asked as they walked toward the elevator.

"Good question. We need to figure out who hired Summers—that's the only thing we have to go on at this point."

"I might be able to help," Gideon said as they road down to the basement lab.

"Really? How?"

"You said he met with a mysterious 'uncle' at the Actors Studio, right?"

Kate nodded. "Uncle Roger."

"Well, I did some searching and discovered that there are some traffic cameras on Tremont Street. I went through the tapes and I might have found your Uncle Roger."

"Really?" Kate's pulse sped up as they spilled out of the elevator and Gideon punched in the code to the lab. "Let's see."

Gideon led her over to the computer where he pulled up a screen that showed the sidewalk outside the Actors Studio. He fiddled with the settings, reversing in fast motion.

"Watch here." He pointed at the door to the building and Kate watched as it swung open and two men walked out. One of them was Caleb Summers.

"That's him!" Kate watched the two men carefully. She could see the tension in Caleb as the two stopped to talk. Then the other man pointed to the left and they both took off in that direction with Caleb sneaking a furtive glance behind him as they walked.

"Do you recognize him?" Caleb asked.

"No." Kate chewed her bottom lip. "When was that?"

Gideon pointed to the timestamp on the bottom. "Last Tuesday—two days before you went to the Antarctic."

"That's got to be Uncle Roger," Kate said. "I wonder what they were saying. Can you zoom in?"

Gideon shook his head. "Sorry, that's as close as it gets. But I could try to run his face through the recognition software."

"Yes. Please do that," Kate said. "I think I'll go catch up on some of the paperwork piling up in my office while it runs."

"Okay, I'll text you if anything comes up."

"Thanks," Kate said as she turned toward the door. "Oh, and Gideon?" she turned back around to face him.

"Yes?" He looked up from the computer screen.

"Let's not tell Mercedes about this just yet. I don't want word to get to the FBI that we have another lead until we check it out thoroughly."

Gideon nodded and returned his attention to the computer.

And after I've had a chance to get a head start, she thought as she exited the lab.

***

Kate spent the rest of the day catching up on the paperwork that was piled in a two-foot tall tower on her desk. *Having an assistant to deal with this stuff would be really nice*, she thought as she worked her way through the pile. Paperwork wasn't her strong suit—she'd rather be out in the field chasing down bad guys and retrieving stolen artifacts.

It was almost suppertime when she finished. She took the expense reports Mercedes had nagged her about earlier in the day straight up to the assistant, hoping to catch a glimpse of Max in his office.

"He's not in," Mercedes said, without even looking up from her computer, as soon as Kate appeared in the doorway.

"Oh, well, I finished the expense reports." Kate slapped the papers on her desk and Mercedes cocked a perfectly plucked brow at her.

"I hope the receipts are legible this time." She picked up the pile and leafed through.

Kate grimaced. The last time she'd done an expense report the receipts had gone through the wash a few times and almost all the ink had washed out. Kate turned to leave, then stopped and turned back.

"Have you met with the FBI lately about the ruby case?" Kate asked.

Mercedes' long red fingernails stopped their clickety-clacking on the keyboard and she looked up at Kate. "Not since last week, why? Do you have something you would like me to relay to them?"

"No. I was just wondering if they told you anything more." Kate knew there was more, she could tell by what Ace had said at the station. She'd wondered why he was holding things back, but maybe he'd told Mercedes and she hadn't mentioned it yet.

"Nope, nothing more than what you already know." Mercedes dismissed Kate by turning back to her computer and Kate cast a longing glance at Max's office door before heading out into the hall.

On her way down the hall, she called Gideon. "Anything yet?"

"Nope." Gideon's voice came over the phone. "I'll keep it running though. Could take all night."

"Okay. Thanks." Kate hung up and made her way to her car.

She noticed the tail only a few miles into her drive. The FBI certainly wasn't wasting any time following her around. She drove slowly the rest of the way so they could keep up. When she pulled into the parking spot, she couldn't help but shoot a smug smile in their direction as she palmed the tracking device in her pocket.

They sped off down the road and Kate figured they wouldn't waste time sitting outside her apartment. They had the device on the car, or so they thought, so they could find out where she was any time they wanted.

Kate didn't realize how tired she was until she got into her apartment. She searched the fridge for food and found only ketchup, half a can of tuna and some milk. The tuna she was saving for Archimedes. The milk was sour so she poured it out. The ketchup she squeezed onto some bread then layered on some potato chips and topped it off with another piece of bread to make a sandwich. It wasn't exactly fine cuisine, but she had to admit it went pretty well with the pink zinfandel she was drinking.

She sat on her couch to think about the day's events.

Ace Mason had wanted her in there for something—he knew she didn't kill Summers, so why pull her in? Had he wanted to warn her there was something more dangerous, or just insult her? She got the feeling it wasn't just about the ruby. But what else could it be about?

Of course, it *had* been a convenient time to plant the tracking device on her car, but as Gideon had pointed out, they really could have done that almost anywhere.

Kate glanced around her apartment uneasily. Had they used the time she was being questioned to search her apartment? She wouldn't put it past them. She'd participated in similar searches when she'd been with the bureau.

Her thoughts drifted to Mercedes LaChance. Was Mercedes telling her the truth when she asked if she'd learned anything more from Mason? There wasn't any indication she was lying, and why would she? She'd have nothing to gain so it probably was true Mason hadn't told Mercedes about whatever it was he was holding back from Kate.

And just why was Mason the one to deal with Mercedes anyway? When Kate was with the FBI, they had someone with lower rank as the liaison.

Why would Ace be doing that personally now? Maybe he was doing it to spend time with the pretty assistant. *She wouldn't put it past him*, Kate thought as she pushed away a pang of jealousy.

Meow!

Kate turned her attention to the window where the gray-striped cat was rubbing his face against the edge of the fire escape and looking in at her with his big yellow eyes. Her lips turned up in a smile as she raced over to the window to let him in.

"Hi Archimedes." She bent down to pet the cat. His ears were cold and she rubbed them, then petted him under the chin eliciting a deep purr.

She went into the kitchen, the cat close on her heels, and pulled the can of tuna out of the fridge. Spooning the cat food onto a plate, she set it on the floor. Archimedes sniffed at it a few times and then hunkered down in front of it taking leisurely, dainty bites.

As the cat ate, Kate got out a tube of superglue. Taking the tracking device from her pocket, she dabbed the glue on, then pressed it to the cat's collar holding it there as the cat ate so it would adhere properly.

Once the cat was done eating, she let him sit in her lap while she finished her glass of wine. Archimedes didn't usually stick around long, and tonight was no exception. After an hour, he was ready to go back out. Kate opened the window for him, and held back a giggle as she watched him slip outside, the tracking device held securely on his collar.

That'll teach Ace Mason to try to put one over on Kate Diamond, she thought as she watched the cat wind his way down the fire escape and through the alley.

***

Ace Mason stared at the blinking green light on the computer screen in front of him.

"Where the heck is she going?" Mick Mulcahey, his partner, frowned at the screen, then looked over at Ace.

Ace let out a chuckle as the green light continued to zigzag through the back alleys of Boston.

"Should we get someone to tail her?" Mick asked.

"Nah, that's not her."

"What?" Mick's ginger-haired eyebrows mashed together as he looked at Ace. "But that's the signal from the tracking id we put in her car." He glanced back at the screen. "How is she even getting her car down some of those streets?"

"She's not," Ace said as he pulled over his laptop and typed something bringing up another screen similar to the one he'd been looking at except the green light wasn't moving around.

Mick looked over at the screen. "What's that? Another tracker?"

"I knew Kate was too smart not to suspect we'd tagged her with a tracking device. So I had Emmy sew another device into the lining of her purse while I was questioning her." Ace tapped at the light on his screen. "This is where she really is ... or her purse anyway—and I've never known her to go anywhere without her purse."

A fist closed around Ace's heart as he thought about Kate. He'd been surprised today that she looked as good, no—better, than he'd remembered. And she still wore that lily of the valley scent that drove him crazy. He'd thought after all this time his feelings for her would have faded ... but they hadn't.

Mick's laughter pulled him out of his thoughts. "So the one under her car was just a decoy. She finds that one and doesn't bother to look anywhere else. That's pretty good ... I guess that's why you're the boss."

Ace looked sharply at Mick and Mick cringed. "Sorry. I'm used to you being the boss."

Ace wasn't the boss anymore and it stung to think about why. He'd done a good job, or so he thought. But after the Damien Darkstone incident, the bureau hadn't liked the way he'd stuck up for Kate and they'd shown their displeasure by knocking him down a few notches in rank.

"No worries, Mick. It's not a big deal," Ace said sincerely. It really wasn't a big deal. The job was pretty much the same except less paperwork and someone else made all the hard decisions. Actually, maybe things were better now that he wasn't the boss.

Both men stared at the stationary light for a while then Mick broke the silence. "So, where is she now?"

Ace looked at the address. He knew it well. "At home. Probably all tucked in for the night."

"And this?" Mick angled his head at the monitor with the moving dot.

Ace squinted at the screen.

"I think she put it on a cat." He chuckled. Probably that striped cat that always came to Kate's window. He had to hand it to her; it was pretty clever to stick the tracer on the cat. Another agent, one that didn't know Kate as well, might have been fooled into going on quite the wild goose chase.

Mick stretched out a yawn. "So we probably don't need to sit here and monitor these.

"Right," Ace said, wondering why he couldn't take his eyes off the dot on the screen. Probably because he wanted to make sure that Kate didn't slip away without him being able to follow her. But not because he wanted to recover the Millennia Ruby first. Ace had a hunch there was a lot more going on here than just the theft of an expensive gemstone and, if his hunch was correct, keeping an eye on Kate could mean the difference between life and death.

"What do you think she'll do next?" Mick stood and grabbed his coat from the back of the chair.

"Who knows, with Kate it could be anything ... I just hope whatever it is, she brings that purse with her."

Chapter Eighteen

Kate woke the next morning in a tangle of sheets. She'd had the dream again except this time the FBI director was taking Ace Mason's badge, which made her feel vindicated ... and a little sad.

Pushing her coppery curls out of her face, she tried to banish any thoughts of the handsome FBI detective. She'd spent the last year training herself *not* to think of him and she'd be damned if one little visit to FBI headquarters would ruin all her hard work.

She showered, blow-dried her curls so that they hung long past her shoulders, then made an attempt to swipe on some makeup. She didn't know why she was taking such pains with her appearance, but it certainly wasn't because she thought she might see Ace Mason again.

Throwing on jeans and an ivory silk blouse, she grabbed her navy blue pea coat and purse and headed over to the museum.

Gideon was in the lab, bent over one of the tables as usual. He hadn't texted her, so she assumed the facial recognition program was still running. He turned around at the sound of the door opening and greeted her with a smile. "Hi."

"Hi." Kate noticed he wasn't wearing a sweater vest. She wondered if her nagging was finally getting to him as she eyed his attire, which consisted of a gray t-shirt with a dark slate colored graffiti type design trailing down one side from shoulder to hem. The shirt was loose over black jeans. Kate suddenly felt uneasy as her eyes lingered on his shirt—who knew Gideon had such broad shoulders and muscular biceps?

"Is something wrong?" His wide green eyes stared at her from behind the thick glasses.

"No, Sorry." Kate shook off the strange feeling. She felt odd, like she'd been checking out her brother. "Nice shirt."

"Thanks. I'm trying to get away from the sweater vests," he said with a wink.

Kate glanced over at the computers. "Did the facial recognition software find a match for Uncle Roger?"

Gideon's face fell. "I'm afraid not. It finished running about a half hour ago."

"It didn't find anything? Is that possible?"

"Sure, if the guy doesn't have a license or has never been arrested … or he could have had surgery to change the way he looks." Gideon crossed over to the computers and brought up the still shot of Summers talking to Uncle Roger they'd fed into the software. "The picture isn't that great either, so it could be that he's in the database, but the software couldn't match him since we only have a side view."

Kate felt her stomach sinking as she looked at the computer and realized that Gideon was right. The picture was fuzzy and only showed one side of the guy's face ... but it was the best one they had.

Kate sunk into a chair. "Now what do we do?"

Gideon rubbed his chin in response and Daisy jumped up into her lap. Kate stroked the dog's fur for comfort.

"We could look through some of the databases manually, but it would take a long time," Gideon offered. "If he's the one who hired Summers, he might have an arrest record ... maybe the software couldn't match him because of the angle of his face. We could look at the pictures ourselves."

Kate screwed up her face. She didn't want to be sitting in front of the computer looking at pictures when she could be out *doing* something.

"That sounds like it could take forever," Kate said. "But you might be on to something. If he *is* the one who hired Summers to steal the ruby, he's probably a jewel thief himself or associated with that business ... and who do we know that knows all the jewel thieves in existence?"

Gideon snapped his fingers and pointed at Kate. "Your parents!"

"Exactly," Kate said. "Can I call them on Skype from here?"

"Of course." Gideon walked over to a computer at the end of the table and Kate followed. Sitting down in front of the computer, Kate logged into Skype, initiated the call to her mother and crossed her fingers that Carlotta was near her computer or had her phone.

After a few rings, Carlotta's face filled the screen. "Katie! How are you?"

"Great Mom, how about you?"

"Wonderful. We're just having a little gathering. Say hi to everyone." Carlotta must have answered on her cell phone or iPad, which she now pointed away from her giving Kate a view of "the gathering." Kate saw the familiar poolside setting of *Golden Capers*. The thatched roof Tiki bar was in full swing with Sal at the blender and a dozen senior citizens in Hawaiian shirts milling around with colorful plastic palm tree stemmed drink glasses in their hands.

"Everyone, say hi to Kate." Kate heard Carlotta's voice then the Hawaiian shirt-wearing seniors turned to wave and say their hellos. Kate knew all of them and her heart warmed—they were like family.

"You're drinking already?" Kate's brow creased as she looked at her watch. "It's only nine in the morning."

Carlotta's face reappeared on the screen. "It's just mimosas. Nothing too strong."

Vic's face appeared on the screen, pushing Carlotta's out of view. "When you're retired like us, time doesn't really mean anything."

Kate raised a brow at Gideon who laughed. Gideon had been down to her parents' place a few times and really liked the older folks down there. He'd especially bonded with a few of them who were geeky inventors just like himself.

"I wish we were there," he said.

"Is that Gideon?" Carlotta grabbed the phone from Vic with a dizzying movement before her face reappeared on the screen. She squinted at the display. "It is! Hi Gideon."

"Hi, Mrs. D." Gideon leaned toward the screen and waved. "Mr. D. ... and everyone else."

"So, how's the ruby search going?" Vic's voice boomed out of the computer.

"Well, that's kind of why we're calling," Kate said.

"I'm sure Gideon was able to verify the one you stole was a fake," Carlotta said confidently. "Did you locate the real one?"

"Yes, it was a fake, Mrs. D," Gideon said. "Did Sal get his thumb back?"

"Oh, yes." Carlotta panned the camera toward Sal again, then yelled, "Sal, how's your thumb?"

Sal smiled and gave them the thumbs up. "Just like new. I appreciate the little addition you did, Gideon."

Kate mashed her brows at Gideon. "Addition?"

Gideon shrugged. "I just made it a little handier by retrofitting a small can opener, screwdriver and knife into the prosthetic. They fold inside like a pocket knife—you can't even tell they are there."

"Yeah. Check it out." Sal held up his thumb and pressed on the thumbnail. A small can opener popped out of the side and Sal used it to pierce a hole in a can of coconut milk. He grinned then slid the opener back in, holding the thumb closer to the cell phone to show how it looked like a normal thumb. "Really comes in handy."

Kate laughed and waved to Benny who had stuck his head into the picture and was waving at her before the screen spun around again showing Carlotta and Vic.

"So, back to the ruby search," Carlotta said. "We actually have some intel that might be of use to you."

"Really?" Kate's brows shot up. "Spill."

"Crowder didn't go underground, and he swears he didn't have anything to do with the theft." Carlotta lifted the paper umbrella out of her drink to reveal a wedge of pineapple, which she chewed thoughtfully. "It could be he doesn't even know the real ruby was stolen and replaced … or if he was in on that, you stealing the fake ruby would be the perfect coverup for him. But according to our sources, he didn't know anything about either."

"But whoever stole the real ruby must have had inside help," Gideon said. "And apparently Crowder wasn't the one chasing Kate and Sal, so there's another party involved."

"We think we figured out how they stole the real ruby," Kate added, then explained how she traced Nguyen's fake identity to Summers and found the disguise and the big deposit in his bank account.

"Why would someone go to all that trouble?" Vic asked taking a sip from his glass. "Did you question this Summers character?"

Kate sighed. "Unfortunately, he's dead.

"Oh, that could be a problem," Carlotta said. "Do you have any other leads?"

"Just one and it's kind of sketchy, but it's the only thing I've got." Kate told them about Uncle Roger and how the facial recognition software didn't find a match. "But the picture's kind of fuzzy and it's not a head on view, so I was wondering if you guys would take a look to see if you recognized him."

"Of course," Carlotta and Vic said at the same time, then glanced at each other and giggled like teenagers.

Kate looked up at Gideon. "Can we show them the picture on the screen?"

"Yep." Gideon gently pushed her out of the way to take over the keyboard. A few keystrokes later, Carlotta and Vic were looking at the picture of "Uncle Roger".

From her screen, Kate saw them glance at each other and then Carlotta said. "That looks like Jimmy Benedetti, don't you think? You know the one who used to wear those crazy shoes."

"Crazy shoes?" Kate asked.

"Yeah, what were they?" Carla scrunched her face up then snapped her fingers. "Testoni. They were made out of some kind of alligator and had a gold and diamond buckle. He wore them all the time, said they were supposed to last forever."

"Yeah, I guess they cost over thirty G's," Vic said. "He really stuck out in those shoes, which I never understood because most bad guys want to blend in. But I guess we all have our quirks. That's definitely him though ... and he's wearing the shoes."

Kate looked at the shoes of the man in the picture. They did look pretty fancy—she could even see a glint of light bouncing off one of the buckles.

"The strange thing is that he's not a jewel thief," Carlotta added. "Which makes me wonder why he would be mixed up in this."

Vic's voice was serious. "He's a real bad guy, Kate. You'd better be careful if you're going to get mixed up with him. He's been associated with some violent criminals."

Kate pushed away a tingle of fear—she wasn't afraid of bad guys. "You wouldn't happen to know where I can find him, would you?"

"We don't actually keep tabs on these people. But we'd love to help if we can," Carlotta said. Some of the other seniors had gathered around to listen in and Kate could hear them murmuring excitedly. Kate knew they all did want to help—apparently, it got boring sitting around having parties all the time.

"You've been a big help already," Kate said. "Now that I know who he is, it'll make it easier to track him down."

"Okay, Kitten. Don't make a move without letting us know," Vic said.

"I won't Dad," Kate answered. "I'll call you with my game plan as soon as I know what it is."

"And don't forget to let us know if we can help." Kate heard Benny yell from behind her folks as she ended the call.

Gideon was already busy typing furiously into the other computer. "I'm going to do a look-up on Benedetti and see if I can get a better picture of him. Then we can feed that into the system and see if he's taken a plane anywhere."

"You can do that?"

"Yeah, the facial recognition software searches the airport databases and they have pictures on file for every passenger," Gideon said. "I wouldn't be able to tell if he traveled by bus, but I might be able to get a match from a car rental."

Kate stared at the computer watching the numbers and images fly by at a dizzying speed while the software did its job.

She wondered if Jimmy Benedetti had the ruby. Her mother had said he wasn't a jewel thief so most likely he was working for someone else. For now though, he was her only lead and she'd have to find him in order to get to the ruby. No matter how much of a violent criminal he was.

"You're not going to go after this guy, are you?" Gideon looked at Kate with genuine concern.

Kate shrugged. "I think I have to. He's our only lead and he probably knows where the real Millennia Ruby is."

"But, your parents said he was violent. Maybe Max was right ... your job is to find out who stole items from the museum and, if you can, retrieve them. There's nothing in your job description that says you have to chase violent criminals to do that." Gideon glanced at Kate. "Maybe you *should* leave that part to the FBI ... or at least consider working with them."

Kate felt anger rise up in her chest. *Didn't anyone think she could handle this job?*

She pierced Gideon with a look. "In case you don't remember, *I* used to be the FBI. I think I have the skills to handle one little bad guy. Besides, last I heard, my job was to get back the *real* ruby and that's exactly what I plan to do— no matter how many violent criminals I have to cross paths with in order to do it."

Chapter Nineteen

Benedetti hadn't traveled under his real name, but the computer matched his picture to a man that had boarded a flight from Boston to the Bahamas two days before.

*It was too close for coincidenc*e, Kate thought. Benedetti had to be involved with Summers and the ruby theft, so she raced home and packed a bag, happy to be including more tropical attire this time.

On the way to the airport, she called her parents, who reminded her that they could get to Bermuda by boat in a matter of hours. And the residents at *Golden Capers* had plenty of boats. They'd happily meet her there.

Mercedes had been able to get her on a plane leaving Logan Airport right away and Kate worked on chewing her fingernails to nubs while she sat impatiently in her seat during the two-and-a-half-hour flight.

The plane landed smoothly and Kate congratulated herself on having the foresight to stuff as much as she could into her purse and carry-on bag so she didn't have to wait for them to unload the baggage from the plane. She was out the door and hailing a cab to the nearest hotel before the first piece of luggage hit the carousel.

Gideon had gotten a lead that Benedetti had taken a cab from the airport to a marina so Kate checked into her room then changed into tan capris, a white tank top and white flat sandals. It felt good to be wearing summer clothes even if her summer tan had faded and her arms and legs where winter-white.

The marina was in St. George's harbor—too far to walk, but Kate had noticed a Scooter rental next to the hotel, so she picked out an environmentally friendly electric scooter and headed toward the marina, remembering to save the receipt for the expense report Mercedes would eventually demand from her.

Kate drank in the warm sunshine and salty ocean breeze as she navigated the winding Bermuda roads. The landscape fell away to her right and she could see the aqua-colored waters of St. George harbor, dotted with boats. The faint cry of gulls filled her ears as she sped past coral colored buildings, her heart racing with the awkwardness of driving on the left hand side of the road as she pushed the scooter as fast as it could go.

The marina was small with three long docks, each containing about fifteen boat slips. Kate parked her scooter and walked into the office.

A stocky man with a beard sat behind the counter. Kate gauged him to be about fifty years old with a bit of a beer belly and a red nose to match. He looked up from the papers on his desk and raised a bushy eyebrow at her.

Kate smiled her most flirtatious smile. "Hi. I'm looking for a friend of mine. He has his boat docked here."

"Name?"

"Benedetti."

The man turned to the keyboard on his right and tapped on the keys. His eyes narrowing at the screen. "Nope. No one here by that name."

Kate pulled a fifty-dollar bill and the picture of Benedetti out of her pocket. She slid them across the counter to him with the fifty on top.

"He might have been using a different name … he's going through a messy divorce." She tapped on the picture. "Do you recognize him?"

The man pocketed the fifty, and then squinted at the picture. "Yeah, that looks like Mr. James." He tapped on the keyboard again. "His boat is in slip nine. Middle row."

"Thanks," Kate said, taking the picture back and putting it in her pocket.

The man nodded as Kate turned and made her way to the door. Outside, she glanced toward the docks. This wasn't the spiffiest marina in Bermuda and the boats were smaller in size. Sailboats and motor boats. A few very small run-down yachts. She made her way to the middle dock and started walking down it, her heart sinking as she got closer to slip number nine.

It was empty.

Kate stood at the empty slip and stared into the harbor. Where did he go? Did he have the ruby or was it already hidden or sold? She stepped down onto the part of the dock that would lead to the side of the boat, if there had been a boat there. A rope was piled up next to a post and she bent down to inspect it. She wasn't even sure what she was looking for. Any type of clue as to where Benedetti was taking the ruby, she supposed.

There was nothing on the dock or in the water that looked like a clue. Kate would have to come up with something else.

Maybe someone in one of the other boats knew where Benedetti was? Kate spun around to survey the boats docked nearby. They appeared empty except for a small fishing boat across the dock and two slips up. A man sat on the deck, tackle box at his feet, soda can in his hand—and he was staring straight at *her*.

"Ahoy there." Kate waved at the man and started up the dock toward him.

He lifted his chin at her. "Hi there."

Kate studied the man as she approached. Dark skin, dark hair and dark eyes—brooding. Not very friendly. She decided to keep her distance so she stopped on the main dock.

"I was looking for Mr. James. He docks his boat there." Kate turned to point at the empty slip.

"Yep." The man sipped his soda.

"Do you know where he went?" Kate squinted into the sun that was hanging low in the sky right behind the man. It would be dark soon and she should probably speed up her investigation.

"I couldn't say." His eyes drilled into hers. "What's your business with him?"

"Oh, just an old friend." Kate saw something she didn't like in his eyes. She looked down and noticed he was tying a fly onto his rod. Which was strange, because one rarely used flies in deep sea fishing—and never with the type of rod he was tying it onto.

She backed down the dock. "Okay, then I'll be going. Thanks."

The man stood and Kate backed away faster.

"What's your name?" He called after her. "I'll tell him you stopped by."

"Oh thanks. That's okay," Kate called over her shoulder. As she hurried down the dock, she cast one last uneasy glance at him and noticed he was staring after her, a cell phone held firmly to his ear.

Kate practically ran back to the scooter, but just as she was about to hop on, she noticed a little open-air bar next to the water. It looked like they served drinks and light meals. That sure would be a convenient place to eat if you had a boat docked here ... especially if you were a wanted criminal who didn't want to traipse around town.

Kate glanced back at the dock and the fisherman had sat back down, his attention on his fishing gear again.

Suddenly she was very thirsty.

***

The smell of fried conch made Kate's mouth water as she slid onto one of the barstools. The bartender, a dark skinned woman in her mid-thirties, was serving a beer to the man who sat two stools down from Kate. He was the only other person sitting at the bar itself, but half the small square tables that sat under the roof of the open-air bar were full with laughing, boisterous customers.

"What'll you have?" The bartender asked with a wide smile.

"Lemonade." Kate didn't feel confident enough to drive the scooter on anything stronger than that.

"Comin' right up."

Kate watched a waitress bring a big plate of fried food to a table and contemplated ordering some herself. The small pack of pretzels she'd eaten on the plane hadn't been very filling. She checked her watch. Her parents would be here soon and she should probably wait for them before making any dinner decisions.

The bartender came back with a large glass loaded with ice and lemonade and Kate took a sip.

"I'm Emmie," The bartender said. "Are you docked here?"

Kate glanced back at the dock. "Oh, no. I was just visiting a friend ... or at least trying to."

Emmie gave her a quizzical look and Kate pulled the picture from her pocket. "His boat wasn't there and, well, we're kind of worried about him," Kate said, showing the picture to the bartender. "Have you seen him?"

Emmie's expression hardened. "Oh, yeah. I've seen him."

Kate raised a brow. "Oh?"

"Yeah, he's been in the past few nights." Emmie leaned toward Kate. "Honestly, I have to tell you he's kind of a loudmouth."

Kate grimaced. "I know. That's why we're worried about where he is."

Emmie nodded. "Yeah, I can understand that. He was here last night and caused a ruckus."

"About what?"

"Believe it or not, it was about his shoes."

"His shoes?"

"Yeah, he had these fancy shoes he was bragging about. But last night, he came in and the shoes were all messed up. Someone commented on it and he had a fit and stormed out of here. He's real touchy about those shoes, I guess."

"Do you know where he went?" Kate asked hopefully.

"No, but since you're his friend and all ..." Emmie bent down looking for something under the bar. She stood back up and slapped something on the bar in front of Kate. "Give him these damn shoes. When he had his little fit last night, he threw them across the bar and left them here."

Kate stared at the shoes. They were the fancy shoes from the photo—the Testoni's. Soft alligator with a gold buckle. Tiny gems winked in the buckle—diamonds, if her parents were correct.

She could see why he would like the shoes; they were beauties, except for one thing. The bottoms and sides were encrusted with bird poop and feathers. Which made Kate wonder, just where had Jimmy Benedetti been with those shoes?

Chapter Twenty

Kate raced back to the hotel with the shoes. She couldn't wait to call Gideon. He might have a way to track the boat via satellite and, since he was such a bird nut, maybe he'd be able to determine something about the bird poop on the shoes. At the very least, he could get a picture of the sole of the shoe. Maybe he could match that to some footprints that would lead them somewhere. Kate knew she was grasping at straws, but straws were all she had.

She returned the scooter and was walking happily along, swinging a shoe in each hand when two shadowy figures came out of nowhere. She felt a viselike grip on each of her elbows. Adrenalin shot through her and she tried to jerk her arms free, but a dark car pulled to the curb and the men shoved her inside.

"Hey, just what do you think you are doing?" Kate's heart thumped against her ribs as she glared at the men who had slid into the backseat on either side of her while the car sped off down the road.

One of the men held out a badge. "Police, Ma'am. We need to ask you some questions."

"Questions?" Kate narrowed her eyes. "About what? I didn't do anything wrong."

One of the men raised a thick dark eyebrow at her. "Oh, no? How about messing with a federal investigation?"

"Federal investigation?" Kate stiffened her spine. "I'm an insurance investigator here on official business myself," she said thinking she really had to get an official badge that she could flash during times like these.

The two men exchanged a glance.

"Insurance investigator?" The man on her right said.

"That's right," Kate replied turning to her right to look at him.

"From where?" The man on her left said.

Kate swiveled her head in his direction. "The *Ritzholdt Museum.*"

"And just what are you investigating?"

Kate swiveled her head back to the man on the right. "The theft of the Millennia Ruby," she said, refraining from adding 'so there'.

"So why were you nosing around at the marina?" This from the man on the left.

"Nosing around? I was investigating a *lead.*" Kate swiveled her head toward him again. "We have reason to believe the person that stole the ruby has a boat there."

Kate noticed with satisfaction that this caused both men to look confused, but they didn't have a chance to grill her further because just then the car screeched to a halt in front of the police station. Or at least she hoped the nondescript building in the middle of nowhere was a police station.

The men opened the doors and yanked her out, which was fine with Kate because her neck was starting to hurt from looking back and forth between them. They ushered her into the building, then down a long hallway where they shoved her into a chair in front of a woman who took her purse, watch, sandals and Benedetti's shoes.

The woman put the items in a box, recording each piece on paper. She seemed bored by the whole thing, although she did lift a brow and look at Kate strangely when she got to the bird poop encrusted Testonis.

When she was done, the bushy-browed man from the car brought her to a room down the hall.

"Someone will be in to talk to you shortly," he informed her before closing—and loudly locking —the door.

***

For the second time in so many days, Kate found herself on the wrong side of the interrogation table.

She sat down in the folding chair, tapping her fingers impatiently on the cold metal tabletop. After a while, she looked at her watch, but of course, only found her bare arm. They'd taken her watch, her purse and the Testoni shoes. She hoped they weren't going to keep the shoes because she had a feeling they held an important clue.

After what seemed like an hour—but was probably only ten minutes—the lock finally clicked again and the door opened.

Kate glanced up hopefully. She was sure once she talked to whoever was in charge, they'd let her go. Maybe she'd even be able to get information out of *them*.

But the man who came through the door wasn't some benign officer in charge who would ask a few questions, then apologize and cut her loose. No, it was someone much less agreeable. Someone who made her stomach churn and her pulse race with anger—Ace Mason.

Kate felt her hope deflating as she watched him walk around to her side of the table, a smug smile on his face. She noticed he'd traded his thermal shirt for a navy blue t-shirt, which showed off his muscular biceps and gave just a peak of the bottom of his armband tattoo.

"What are *you* doing here?" Kate demanded.

How had he tracked her down?

"I might ask you the same." Ace cocked an eyebrow at her as he leaned his hip on the table.

"I'm following a lead on the ruby," she said. "I guess you couldn't come up with your own leads so you followed me."

Ace chuckled. "If you want to think that, go ahead. The truth is that I *do* have my own leads."

"What leads? People spying on me? The guys that pulled me in?"

That would explain how they found me so fast, Kate thought.

"No." Ace leaned forward. "Actually the guys that pulled you in are investigating Benedetti for something else. They had an undercover guy at the marina and when he saw you asking around, he figured they'd better find out who you were."

Kate's mind flashed to the guy with the fly fishing setup on the boat. Of course, that explains why he would be using the wrong rig ... and his quick phone call.

She leaned back and crossed her arms over her chest. "So where do you fit in?"

"I'm part of *that* investigation too. You know how it is in the FBI, sometimes you gotta work more than one case."

Kate narrowed her eyes at Ace. "So how does that investigation tie into the ruby theft?"

Ace shrugged. "That's not really your concern."

"It sure as hell is. Anything that's relevant could lead me to the ruby. You can't hold that information back on me ... you have a deal with the museum."

"I'm fully aware of my deal and I don't intend to hold back anything that is relevant to retrieving the ruby. Do you?"

Kate's heart skipped. She couldn't exactly say she'd been forthcoming with information. Oh, she'd pass it along eventually, but she just wanted a teensy weensy head start.

"I believe I've passed along everything I know." Kate winced as she thought about the Testoni shoes. She comforted herself with the fact that she didn't exactly know that they had anything to do with the case. So telling Ace about them would be premature. And it wouldn't be nice to send the FBI off on a wild goose chase, now would it?

"Good. So, then I guess we're both up to date on the case," Ace said.

"Good. Can I go now?"

Kate glanced back up at Ace and she saw his face harden. His gray eyes held hers, causing her breath to catch in her throat.

"Listen Kate, This Benedetti guy ... he's a tough criminal. You don't want to get mixed up with him. Let me get the ruby—you've done a good job following the trail, but I can pick it up from here."

Kate's stomach flip-flopped. Ace was being sincere—she could see it in his eyes. He really was concerned about her getting hurt. Then she remembered the whole business with Damien Darkstone, and how she'd *thought* he was sincere then, too.

Kate narrowed her eyes at him. "Oh, no. I'm not falling for that one. You just want to be the one to get the ruby."

Ace rubbed his hands through his short hair. "Kate, it's not about that. I don't care about the ruby ... I just don't want you to get hurt."

"Oh sure, Just like you didn't want me to get hurt two years ago." Tears pricked the backs of Kate's eyes and she looked away. "Well, I'm not stupid enough to fall for your empty promises twice."

"Kate, what went down two years ago didn't happen the way you think it did," Ace said quietly.

Kate's heart pinched at his words. *What did he mean by that?*

She didn't give herself time to think about it. That was the past and she wanted to focus on the future. And finding the ruby.

She turned back to him, a triumphant gleam in her eye. "Well, I don't know what you *hoped* to accomplish by pulling me in here, but I'll tell you one thing you *did* accomplish. You've verified that I'm on the right track ... because if I wasn't, you wouldn't be so keen to get me to drop the case and go home."

Chapter Twenty One

Kate refused Ace's insistent offers to drive her back to her hotel and called a cab instead. She didn't want to have to spend any more time with him than was necessary ... and she didn't want him to see Benedetti's shoes. She figured he wouldn't have taken an interest in the personal items they catalogued when she came to the station and the shoes were at least one clue she wanted to keep to herself.

Her hotel room was nice—not the best but not the worst either. It was high on a hill with a view of the ocean from the balcony. Palm trees and flowering shrubs dotted the property. Her room was decorated in a starfish motif with white and light gold hues. She threw her purse on the couch, then sunk down into its white slip-covered depths.

She'd set her laptop on the coffee table when she'd checked in earlier and she pulled it over toward her and tapped the button to bring it to life. She couldn't wait to call Gideon and see if he could find out where Benedetti had taken his boat.

As she tapped the keys, she wondered how Ace Mason had found her so easily. She remembered the tracking device she'd discovered on her car, her lips curling in a smile as she pictured Ace and his team chasing the cat through the back streets of Boston.

But if the tracking device was on the cat, how did Ace catch up to her so quickly? It didn't make sense that he'd track her and have someone following her in person. Her eyes slid over to the purse lying beside her on the couch.

No, he wouldn't have.

She dived for the purse, dumped the contents on the floor and shoved her hand inside to feel the lining against the side of the purse. Anger bubbled up in her chest when she felt a little bump in-between the silk lining and leather outside of the purse. A quick inspection of the stitching in that area proved her suspicions.

"Damn him!"

"Excuse me?" Gideon's voice sounded from the laptop and Kate turned to it in surprise. She'd been so focused on looking for the bug in her purse she hadn't even noticed the call had gone through.

She shoved the purse at the camera. "It's that damn Ace Mason! He put a tracker in my purse!"

Gideon laughed, which made Kate even madder. "That's sneaky. I can't believe you fell for that, though."

Kate made a face. "I figured when we found the one in my car, that was it. I should have known."

"So he's there in Bermuda?"

"Yes. I just had a little run-in with him. He knows about Benedetti." Kate threw down the purse and leaned toward the computer. "I went to the marina you got the tip on and Benedetti does have a boat there. The slip was empty though. Is there any way you can find out where that boat went?"

Gideon twisted his lips together. "I'm not sure. What's the name of the boat?"

Kate's shoulders slumped. "Crap. I didn't get a name. But I know it was in slip nine, maybe we can zoom in with satellite photo and figure it out?"

"Maybe," Gideon said and Kate could see he was tapping away at the keyboard.

"Oh and I have his shoes," Kate added.

"Pardon?" Gideon raised a brow at the camera.

"The Testonis. Hold on." Kate got up and retrieved the shoes, then held them up to the camera. "These are the shoes my parents said that Benedetti always wore. The bartender at the Tiki bar in the marina said he left them there."

Gideon scrunched up his face. "And she gave them to you?"

Kate grimaced. "I said I was a friend."

"What's that all over them?"

Kate looked at the bottoms of the shoes. "Looks like bird poop and mashed in feathers." She held the side with the most poop on it up to the camera so Gideon could get a close-up. "I was thinking that maybe Benedetti hid the ruby some place with a lot of birds or something."

"Let me see the heel," Gideon said.

Kate shoved the heavily encrusted heel toward the camera.

"Those downy feathers," Gideon said. "Are they bright blue?"

Kate looked at the shoe. "Yes."

Gideon's face lit up and he got busy typing. "Kate, I think I know where Benedetti has been."

"You do?"

"Yes. There's a volcanic island near Bermuda that has a rare type of crow. The Bermudian Blue Crow. In fact, it's called Blue Crow Island." Gideon looked up at Kate. "The blue crow hatchlings have feathers just like those on the shoe."

"So Benedetti might have taken the ruby there to hide it!" Kate said.

"That would explain his shoes," Gideon said. "But why would he want to hide the ruby on an abandoned island?"

Kate's forehead creased as she thought about that. Did she really care why? All she wanted was to bring it back to the museum, what did she care about Benedetti's motives?

"Who cares?" Kate said. "I just need to bring it back. And I know just the people to help me go get it."

***

"Hold on there," Gideon said. "Blue Crow isn't some tropical beach island. It's mostly volcanic rubble and dense undergrowth. It will be rough going … and I think the volcano is still active."

"Maybe we can make some educated guesses as to the most likely places he would hide the ruby and check those first," Kate suggested.

"I can look at satellite photos of the island," Gideon said. "In the meantime, I have some gear that will be perfect for the terrain. I'll send down enough for several people. I assume your parents will be accompanying you."

"Naturally," Kate said. "They are coming over on one of their friends' boats … actually they should be calling any second now."

"Well, you're not going to head over tonight in the dark, I hope," Gideon said. "It will be most dangerous in the dark and I won't be able to send the gear down until tomorrow."

Kate frowned. She was impatient to get there right away, but Gideon did have a point. It would be easier to find the ruby in daylight. And she did have the little problem of Ace Mason, who most likely had someone watching her right now.

"Yeah, you're right," Kate said. "I'll wait until tomorrow and that will give you some time to pull everything together and get some satellite photos of the island. Also, I'm going to need a good disguise to slip past Ace Mason and his posse. I'm pretty sure he'll have someone watching outside my hotel."

"I've got just the thing," Gideon said. "I'll send it down with the gear on the first museum freight flight to that area tomorrow and arrange for courier delivery to your hotel room."

"Perfect." Kate smiled and gave Gideon the thumbs up. "This time tomorrow we could be kicking back and celebrating the recovery of the Millennia Ruby ... and Ace Mason will be standing outside my hotel wondering what happened."

Chapter Twenty Two

Gideon was true to his word and a courier showed up at ten the next morning with a package. Kate's parents had arrived in the evening with a crew of reinforcements from *Golden Capers* and their small yacht was docked a few miles away.

They'd wanted to meet for supper, but Kate had declined. If Ace discovered her parents were here in a boat, he'd have someone watching the boat and then he'd follow them to Blue Crow Island and try to get the ruby first.

Kate figured it was better to stay at the hotel all night and then sneak out in the morning— leaving the tracking device in the hotel room, of course.

She ripped open the box. Inside were special vests, shoes and gloves that were designed for use in the type of rocky, volcanic terrain found on Blue Crow Island. There was also a satellite communication device that looked pretty much like a tricked out wristwatch, which she could use to communicate with Gideon since there were no cell phone towers in range. Gideon had thoughtfully packed enough for the entire crew and included a duffel bag. Kate packed the gear into the bag before changing into a light summer outfit of lavender plaid shorts and a lavender tank top.

There was one more thing in the box—the disguise. It was one of Kate's favorites.

A smile curled on her lips as she tucked her hair up under the long dark red wig. Ace Mason and his cohorts would never recognize her. She'd be able to sneak right past them and all the time, he'd be thinking she was in her room.

Taking out the contact lens case, she made her way to the bathroom, then plopped the sapphire blue lenses into her eyes. She painted her lips with extra deep red, put on a generous amount of lavender eye shadow and plastered mascara on her naturally long lashes. Blinking at her own reflection, Kate had to admit she barely even recognized herself.

Slipping into a pair of lavender cork wedge-heel sandals, she emptied her purse into the duffel bag, which she slung over her shoulder. Heading for the door she shoved a pair of oversized sunglasses on her face, then glanced back once at the empty purse—with the tracking device still intact—opened the door and slipped out into the warm Bermuda sunshine.

She was sure someone from the FBI was watching, but she had no idea who. She kept her head forward—she didn't want to give herself away by looking like *she* was looking for someone looking for *her*. Her eyes though, hidden behind the sunglasses, darted wildly from side to side trying to spot the tail but no one stood out.

The taxi she'd called for pulled up to the curb and she got in, giving the driver the address to the marina where her parent's boat was in. She didn't relax until they were a mile away and her constant backward glances satisfied her that she wasn't being followed.

***

The *High Jinx* was a small fifty-foot Viking convertible yacht owned by Gertie. Kate had sailed on it many times and she recognized the sleek profile as soon as she got out of the cab. The occupants of the yacht, however, did not recognize her, which delighted her to no end. Kate loved it when her disguises did their job, and if she weren't in such a hurry to get to Blue

Crow Island, she would have had her fun with them and played an elaborate charade pretending to be someone else.

But, as it was, she whipped off the wig and sunglasses amidst the shocked look of Sal, Benny, Gertie and Frankie. Her mother and father claimed to have known it was her all along.

"Gideon sent down some equipment to help us navigate the terrain on the island." Kate lifted the bag off her shoulder and swung it onto the bench seat on the back of the boat. Gertie and Frankie went through the motions of untying the boat and pulling it away from the dock.

"Let's go into the salon and take a look." Vic picked up the bag and headed inside. The salon wasn't terribly huge. It had a kitchenette, 'L' shaped leather sofa and a separate dinette. The walls were shiny teak and windows lined three sides, giving Kate a breathtaking view of Bermuda as they sped away into the Atlantic.

Vic tossed the bag on the tan leather couch, then unzipped it, leaned over and took the items out one at a time, lining them up across the sectional.

"These are great. That Gideon really knows how to come through," Vic said sitting down and trying on one of the shoes. "He called me to see what shoe sizes we would need."

"Oh." Kate hadn't thought about that ... good thing she had Gideon to back her up.

Vic continued. "And he gave me the coordinates for this island. Gertie has them programmed in."

"Anyone want a sandwich?" Carlotta had come in and was standing in front of the open fridge.

"Umm ... Maybe we should come up with a plan." Kate looked out the window. They were going pretty fast and would be at the island soon, a plan of action was critical.

"Oh, yeah. We already discussed it. Gideon said the best place to land was the east side of the island. Gertie picked this spot here." Vic walked over to the dinette and pointed to a spot on the map that lay on the table. "We'll split up and search in different directions to cover the most ground, then rendezvous back in two hours and reassess."

"Okay. That sounds good," Kate said feeling a little left out. Wasn't this *her* mission? She should have come up with the plan but, truth be told, she couldn't think of a better one.

"Just what are we looking for, Kate?" Sal had come down from the bridge and was looking in the fridge with Carlotta.

"I guess any sort of hiding place or anything that looks suspicious," Kate said. "A building maybe, or a cave ..."

"But why would he hide the ruby on this deserted island?" Carlotta bit into a turkey on rye. "It just doesn't make sense."

"I know, but Benedetti hired Summers to steal the ruby and Benedetti's trail leads here. So I figure either the ruby is here, or some sort of clue is on the island." Kate shrugged and picked a pickle chip off Carlotta's plate. "We should look for anything out of place; which, I guess on this island, is anything that isn't bird poop, volcanic rock or feathers."

"Land ahoy!" Gertie called down from the bridge and Kate glanced out the window to see a large island up ahead. It was lush with tropical plants and she could see the cone of a volcano sticking up in the middle.

"Okay, There's no dock so we'll take the inflatable ashore," Vic said. "Gertie will drop anchor as close as she can, then we'll inflate the boat and drop it into the water. I brought the trolling motor so we can motor ashore."

"Sounds like a plan," Kate said as she sat on the sectional, ready to change into the special mountain climbing shoes Gideon had sent. Vic lifted the bench on the leather covered banquette and Kate's eyes went wide when she saw what was stored in there—an arsenal of guns. "You don't think we're going to need guns, do you?"

Vic shrugged and Kate looked out the window again.

"There's no one on the island," Kate pointed out. Or was there? If Benedetti's boat wasn't at the marina, then where was he? Would they round the island to find his boat moored somewhere?

The boat slowed to a crawl. They had rounded the island and were on the east side. No other boats were in sight.

"I guess no one else is here," Sal said with a hint of disappointment in his voice.

"We should each take a gun to be on the safe side," Vic said. "It might come in handy if you scare up some kind of animal. It looks pretty dense out there and who knows what kind of creatures lurk in the jungle."

Kate felt a shiver run up her spine. "Gideon said it was full of crows."

"It sure is." Gertie came in wiping something from her arm with Frances right behind her. "Damn things are flying all around up there and pooping all over the boat." She eyed the guns. "Good, I'm gonna go shoot 'em."

"Hold on, there," Carlotta said. "Let's check out the island first. *Then* you can shoot the crows."

They each put on the gear, picked out a gun and headed to the back of the yacht. Vic dragged the inflatable out of its storage spot in one of the specially made lockers on the side of the boat next to the live well, then dropped it over the edge and pulled the chord to inflate it.

The small yacht was shallow so they were able to moor it close to shore. They could have paddled the inflatable in, but Vic set up the trolling motor anyway. The back of the yacht sat low in the water. It was only two feet off the surface, so they only had to sit on the back and swing their legs over to get into the raft.

As they motored over to the sandy beach, Sal took off his shoes and rolled up his khaki green cargo pants, then once they raft was bumping up against the sand, he jumped out of the front. Splashing in ankle-deep water, he pulled the raft up onto the beach so the rest of them could get out without getting their feet wet.

"Thanks Sal." Kate patted him on the back as she jumped out of the raft.

"Don't mention it." Sal sat on the front of the raft and put his shoes and socks back on.

"We should split up to cover more ground. Katie, you, Carlotta, and Sal go to the north. Gertie, Frankie, and I will go to the south," Vic said, looking at his watch. "We'll meet back at the raft in two hours. Then we'll decide what to do next."

"Sounds like a plan," Sal said and they all held out their fists for a group fist bump.

Vic, Gertie and Frankie disappeared into the lush vegetation on the right. "Well, I guess we'd better get started," Carlotta said as she walked toward the giant ferns on the north side of the beach.

"Yep," Kate said. "Oh, wait. I should use this communication gizmo to make sure I can raise Gideon." Kate pressed a button on the watch-like instrument that sat on her wrist, shrugging her shoulders when all she heard was static.

"Is it broken?" Sal asked.

"I'm not sure." Kate pressed the button again. "Gideon? Are you there?"

More static, then "... ate ... er ... me."

"Gideon?"

"Hey Kate ... o hear me?"

"Yes, there's some static ... I think something is interfering with the transmission—let me go to an open area on the beach." Kate walked over by the water, pressing the button again, this time with less static. "Can you hear me?"

"Yes, much better." Gideon's voice came through clear. "Are you on the island?"

"Yes."

"Any surprises?

"Not so far. We just got here."

"Okay, watch out for the rocky slopes," Gideon said, then added. "And the crows; I hear they can be quite vicious."

Kate looked up as a crow flew overhead. "Will do."

"Okay, I'm looking at more satellite photos. I'll let you know if I find anything."

"Okay, over and out," Kate said.

"Right." Gideon's chuckle mixed with static as Kate walked back over to the edge of the trees. "You don't have to say over and out ... you can just say bye."

"Okay, bye," she said, rolling her eyes.

Carlotta raised a brow and held a giant fern out of the way for Kate and Sal to precede her. "Well then, I guess we're going in."

Chapter Twenty Three

Blue Crow Island was hot, humid and hard to navigate. Even with special shoes that helped them cling to the rocky terrain, it was hard to keep from stumbling. Mosquitoes buzzed in Kate's ear as she wiped the sweat out of her eyes. The lush undergrowth made it impossible to see more than five feet in any direction.

"I don't see how we're going to find a ruby in here—you can't *see* anything," Sal complained.

"I think if we get above the vegetation line, we'll be able to look down and then any hiding places might be evident," Carlotta said.

"Caw!"

A crow flew over them and something splattered on a giant leaf beside Kate. The ground was dotted with white splotches of crow poop and there seemed to be more and more birds the higher they climbed. *No wonder Benedetti's shoes had been encrusted with the stuff*, Kate thought as she struggled up the hilly terrain.

"Damn birds." Kate looked up. She could swear the bird was looking down at her. Watching her. Tracking her every movement.

The hairs on the back of her neck prickled and she got that creeped-out feeling that she was being watched. But that was ridiculous, the island was deserted and the crows certainly didn't care what she was doing.

Finally, the plants started to thin and they stopped to rest, sipping from the bottled waters they'd brought in their vests.

"I can see a good part of the island from up here." Carlotta had scurried ahead and was standing on a large boulder that stuck out from the side of the hill. She held her hand up to shade her eyes. "There's nothing but trees, ferns and crows. Are you sure the ruby is here?"

"Well, I'm not exactly sure. But it's all I had to go on." Doubt started to take hold of Kate. What if she was wrong and there was nothing but crow poop here? If she was, she'd just made an awfully expensive trip for nothing.

"We can't possibly search this whole island. It's too dense." Sal had joined Carlotta on the boulder.

"Isn't there someplace obvious that stands out?" Kate asked hopefully, as she climbed up on the boulder. They were right, it would be impossible to search every inch of the island.

She'd hoped once they were here, the hiding place would stick out like a sore thumb.

From her vantage point, she could see the blue waters of the Atlantic and the green vegetation of the island below. Above her, the brown rock top of the volcano loomed toward the sky. Crows circled overhead. She didn't see any place where one would hide a ruby and was wondering why she'd even thought Benedetti would bring it here … but his shoes *proved* that he'd been here and they were the only clue to the ruby that she had.

Just then, her wrist communicator cracked. "… ate … gency … now!"

Kate screwed up her face "Was that Gideon? What did he say?"

Carlotta and Sal shrugged.

Kate stabbed at the button. "Gideon? Come in."

More static. Then "… alk … right away!"

Kate's stomach clenched. The few snippets of voice she'd heard sounded tense. Was Gideon in trouble? Or, more likely Gideon had discovered something about the island that he needed her to know.

"I think Gideon needs to tell us something, but the reception is bad up here." Kate shook the watch, then tapped on it. "Gideon?"

Nothing but static came out.

"It sounded urgent," Carlotta said uncertainly.

"Maybe we should head back down. There's not much to see up here, anyway," Kate said.

"And it's almost time to meet up with the others." Sal jumped down from the boulder, surprisingly fit for an older man and the three of them started back down the thin path they'd made on the way up.

Going down was a lot easier than climbing up and they made it to the beach quickly. Kate could feel the crows watching her the whole time. It made her jittery and even more nervous about Gideon's message. She tried the communication watch again on the beach, but once again, there was nothing but static.

"Oh crap. Gertie's gonna be on the warpath." Kate followed Carlotta's gaze to the bridge of the boat where several crows were perched on the railing preening their bluish black feathers. She grimaced at the white splotches marring the once perfectly polished chrome.

"Jeez, we better go scare them off." Sal motioned for them to hop into the boat.

"Yeah, and I can use the satellite communication to call Gideon," Kate said as she hopped over the inflated edge.

"And I could use dessert," Carlotta added as she joined Kate in the boat.

They motored to the yacht. Sal tied the inflatable off and they all jumped out.

Sal looked at his watch. "The others won't be here for another half-hour so we can keep an eye out for them and come back to pick them up when we see them on the beach."

"Good idea," Kate said as she headed for the salon where there was a computer she could use. The yacht was equipped with satellite access so she could call Gideon on Skype and see what was so urgent.

Sal headed up to the bridge to scare away the crows and Carlotta followed Kate, making a beeline for the fridge while Kate slid into the buttery leather sectional. Pulling the laptop in front of her, she flipped up the screen and looked for Skype.

"Want some pie?" Carlotta asked as she backed out of the fridge with a tin pie plate and then pulled out the drawer for a fork. She leaned against the granite counter and dug into the pie.

"No thanks. I can't find Skype on here … oh here it is." Kate pushed the button and listened to the ring while it tried to connect to Gideon on the other end.

"Kate! Are you all right?" Gideon's concerned face filled the screen.

"Yes, of course," Kate said. *Why wouldn't she be all right?* "The communication device was all static when you called me before. What's so important?"

"Just a sec," Gideon said and she could see him typing furiously on the keyboard. "I developed those pictures you took of the penguins a little while ago."

"Oh great. Did they come out good?" Kate asked wondering why that was so important.

"Yeah fine. It's not that though." A tremor crept into Gideon's voice that set Kate's nerves on edge. "One of the pictures happened to be of the guys that were chasing you. They were on their ski-mobiles at the edge of the glacier."

Kate remembered flying off the glacier on the sky-cycle and randomly taking shots with the camera in the hopes at least one of the pictures would be of the penguins on the iceberg. Apparently, she'd gotten more than that.

"Yeah. So?" she asked, wishing he would get to the point.

"I think one of the guys is that criminal you were after at the FBI. Hold on and I'll put the picture up on your screen."

Kate's brow creased. "What crimina—"

A picture of six men in snowsuits flashed on her screen. They were at the edge of the glacier looking toward the camera. Two of them were sitting on the ski-mobiles, one half-standing and the fourth fully standing. Her blood froze as she studied the one that was standing.

Damien Darkstone.

What did he *have to do with the ruby?*

"Kate, is that him?" Gideon's voice was urgent.

Kate could barely answer. She felt like she'd had the wind knocked out of her. "Yeah, but what would he possibl—"

Smash!

Kate's words were cut short as the glass window beside her shattered. She whipped her head around in time to see a canister spewing colored gas clatter onto the floor.

"Get down!" she yelled across to Carlotta who was already down, the glass window beside her also shattered.

Kate's eyes watered as she choked on the acrid air. Her heart pounded against her ribs.

What was going on?

She could hear Gideon frantically calling her name through the computer as she tried to crawl over to Carlotta to see if she as okay but the air inside the boat was filling with the colored gas making it impossible for her to see ... or breathe.

She heard the power systems on the boat shut down, including the computer. Gideon's frantic voice was silenced. As she gasped in a few final breaths, she thought she heard heavy footsteps but couldn't be sure.

And then everything went dark.

Chapter Twenty Four

"Kate! Open up!" Ace banged his fist on the hotel door, his stomach sinking lower with each passing second.

She wasn't in there.

He should have known when it got to be noon that Kate had given him the slip. He'd been up since one o'clock in the morning, staring at the little green light that represented the tracking device in her purse and it hadn't moved an inch. He thought she was in her hotel room the whole time, but clearly, she must have snuck out and left her purse behind.

"Get the manager to open this door." Ace barked the order at no one in particular and one of the newer members of his team, Jim, took off toward the manager's office.

"She gave you the slip, eh?" Mick raised a brow and Ace had all he could do not to punch him in the face.

"Yeah, looks that way." Ace rubbed his hand through his hair. "I *knew* she wouldn't just sit in her room all morning ... we should have come sooner."

"Aww, don't be so hard on yourself," Mick said as the manager appeared with the keys and a concerned look on his face.

"Is something wrong in there?" the manager asked.

"No, we just want to make sure she's okay," Ace said. It wasn't really a lie ... he did want to make sure she was okay, or at least not hiding in there. And search the room for clues to where she might have gone.

The manager used the key to open the door. Ace pushed his way inside, checking the living room, bedroom and bath quickly. Kate wasn't there but her empty purse was. She'd discovered the tracking device.

"She's not here. Look around to see if there's any clue as to where she might have gone," Ace said as he paced around the living room while Mick and the other two members of his team searched the room.

"Do you think she knows where Darkstone is?" Mick asked.

Ace sighed. "That's the thing. I don't even think she knows *about* Darkstone. She just wants to get the ruby for the museum."

Mick lifted a shaggy brow. "Ahh, so she could be heading straight for danger and not even know it. Why didn't you tell her?"

"Come on, Mick. You know that information was on a strictly 'need to know' basis." Ace's heart squeezed. He *should* have told her anyway. Sure, he'd done his best to try to get her to back off, but she'd thought that had been about the ruby.

If he'd told her Darkstone was somehow involved would she have listened to him? Probably not. But at least she'd have been prepared. As it was he felt like he'd sent her off like a lamb to the slaughter ... and if anything happened to her, he'd never be able to forgive himself.

The others came back into the room. "There's nothing here," Jim said.

"We need to figure out where she went," Ace replied. "We know she was down here tracking Benedetti, so we have to assume she got some kind of lead and took off to follow it."

"We didn't see anyone matching her description leave," Jim said, looking at the other man, Bobby O'Brien, for confirmation. "The only people that left here this morning were an old man and a redhead."

"She must have slipped out the back." Mick had crossed to the sliding glass door and was looking out. "She could have climbed down from here."

"Dammit!" Ace pounded his fist into his thigh. Kate was heading straight into danger and if anything happened to her, it was going to be *his* fault. He couldn't have that on his conscience. Which meant he'd have to figure out where she had gone. Ace could think of only one person that might know exactly where Kate was headed. Could he swallow his pride long enough to call him and find out?

***

"We're just on time to meet Carlotta, Sal and Kate." Vic Diamond peered at his watch as they tromped through the jungle toward the beach where they'd left the raft.

"Good, because I'm hungry," Frankie said.

"Yeah, I hate to say it Vic, but I think this might be a wild goose chase." Gertie looked up as a crow flew over. "Or maybe crow chase would be more appropriate."

Gertie elbowed Frankie in the ribs and they both laughed at her joke. But Vic wasn't laughing. He'd emerged from the bushes onto the sandy beach only to find the inflatable raft was gone.

"What the heck?" The three of them glanced over toward the yacht.

"Will you look at those damn crows?" Gertie waved her arms. "Shoo! Shoo!"

"Wait a minute." Vic stared at the boat, his gut churning. "Something isn't right there."

"Yeah, I'll say, those crows are gonna have it full of poo—"

"The windows," Vic said. "You guys stay here."

Vic heard Gertie suck in a breath before he sprang into action, throwing down his gun, shedding his vest and kicking off his shoes as he ran toward the water.

Even though he was nearing seventy, Vic kept himself in shape. It was nothing for him to swim the thirty feet out to the *High Jinx*. He was running on pure adrenalin—his family could be in there, hurt.

He reached the boat in record speed and hauled himself up into the back deck. A foul smell hung in the air. Vic recognized it right away. Knockout gas. He ran into the salon and, sure enough, the canisters were lying on the ground. The windows had been smashed from the outside.

"Katie! Carlie!" Vic yelled as he ran through the boat searching the two staterooms, the bathroom and the bridge. They were all empty. His family was gone—taken by someone. But who? And why?

Vic's shoulders slumped as he walked back to the raft. It looked like Carlotta had been right—hiding the ruby here didn't make much sense. There had been another motive for bringing the ruby here all along.

Vic wasn't sure exactly what that motive was, but he was sure of one thing ... someone else was on this island and he had to find them. The life of his wife and daughter depended on it.

***

Rushing back to the raft, Vic could see Gertie and Frankie shuffling nervously on the beach.

"They're not here!" he yelled at them. "I'll come get you in the raft."

He jumped into the raft and took off toward the beach. Gertie and Frankie waded out to meet him, and then they headed back to the yacht.

"What happened?" Frankie asked.

"I don't know," Vic said. "It looks like Kate, Carlotta and Sal must have gotten back early. I guess they took the inflatable to the yacht and someone broke in, using some sort of gas, which, I assume, rendered them all helpless and then they took them."

"Took them?" Gertie screwed her face up. "Why?"

"Your guess is as good as mine," Vic said as he swung the raft alongside the back of the boat and tied it off.

"Well, what does it matter?" Frankie shrugged as he climbed onto the yacht. "The way I see it, we got no choice but to just go and take them back."

"Right," Gertie said. "Let's make our plan."

She stormed into the salon and lifted the seat from one side of the dinette to reveal a selection of automatic and semi-automatic weapons.

"This is where I keep the good stuff," she said. "Take your pick."

Vic raised a brow at Frankie as the two men stared into the storage space, which was piled full of various guns. He reached in and picked out a Sig Saur P522 Swat pistol, Frankie grabbed a Glock 18, and Gertie pulled out a semi-automatic pistol and a rifle.

They loaded up with ammunition and Vic slid the satellite map of the island into the center of the dining table.

"I didn't see any place to bring captives while we were out on the island before. I think the best plan is to skirt the north side of the island and look for any caves or houses." Vic traced his finger along the north side of the island. "Then we'll climb up the hill to the top of the volcano and see what we can see."

"We should stick together," Frankie said. "It could be dangerous."

Gertie nodded. "We always worked good in a team this way anyway."

"Right. Let's go." Vic headed toward the back of the boat.

"It might help if we had an idea of who we were looking for or how many of them there are," Gertie said as she loaded the rifle into the raft then jumped in after it.

"Unfortunately, I have no idea who or how many." Vic looked over at Gertie, then noticed something in the ocean just past her shoulder.

He squinted, craning his neck at the small speck that seemed to be getting larger.

Gertie turned to see what he was looking at. "Is that a boat?"

"I think it is," Frankie said.

The three of them stared for a few seconds as the speck got large enough to reveal that it *was* a boat.

"Get your guns ready," Vic said. "It looks like it's headed our way."

***

"Can't this thing go any faster?" Ace leaned on the bow of the small Boston Whaler V hull boat as if his weight pressing forward could add to its speed.

"I'm pushing it as fast as I can. This isn't exactly a speed boat." Jim gave Ace a wry look as he aimed the boat toward the black dot that was starting to take shape as a small island.

Ace's gut churned. The cold spray of the saltwater stung his face. He'd been surprised when Gideon eagerly returned his call, reciting a firsthand account of Kate's attack. Given the circumstances, Gideon had been more than happy to give Ace the exact coordinates of the island. He just hoped it wouldn't be too late by the time he got there.

Ace pressed the binoculars he held to his eyes.

"I think I see the boat." Ace squinted into the lenses. He could barely make out a white dot, which he assumed was the boat Kate had taken. The *High Jinx* Gideon had said the name of it was. A boat owned by one of Kate's parents. Ace pressed his lips together in disapproval—he didn't like the fact Kate often used the ex-thieves and con men on her cases. Even though they all claimed to be retired, he still felt that they operated outside the law and he couldn't condone that.

Adrenalin shot through him as he detected movement on the boat. Was it Kate? Her abductors? He could see three people in the back of the boat. It looked like they were getting into an inflatable raft, but he was still too far away to make out who it was.

Moving the binoculars upwards, he could see the damage to the boat. The windows were broken just as Gideon had said. And what was with all those crows?

Looking back at the raft, he could see the three people were armed with semi-automatic rifle and handguns. But they weren't the people who had taken Kate—he recognized one of them as Kate's father. The others must be two of the retired law-avoiding citizens of *Golden Capers*.

They must be gearing up to find Kate and her mother, he thought.

A hot stab of irritation pierced his gut. He was going to have to work hand in hand with Vic Diamond to get Kate back safely. The thought of it made his fists clench, but there was no other way. Vic was already armed and they could certainly use the help since he had no idea how many people they would be up against.

If Ace wanted to ensure Kate's safety, he'd have to put aside his personal feelings and form an alliance with Vic Diamond.

Chapter Twenty Five

Someone had jabbed a red-hot poker into Kate's head ... or at least it felt that way, Kate thought, as she surfaced from the depths of unconsciousness. Her pounding head seemed like it weighed a ton, too. Which was problematic, since it seemed to be lolling forward, stretching her neck at an uncomfortable angle.

She winced as she made the effort to lift her head, pushing down a wave of nausea.

Where was she?

Kate struggled to remember what had happened, but her memory was fuzzy. Her eyes burned and itched and her sight was blurry. Looking around, she could barely make out that she was in a darkened area with walls made of ... rock? Was she in a cave?

Kate's senses were coming awake now, she felt cold steel biting into her wrists—restraining her. She looked down, her ankles were chained to the legs of a metal chair, her arms twisted and chained behind her. In contrast to the cold steel shackles, the air was warm and tinged with an acrid smell reminiscent of sulfur.

An ear-piercing caw followed by a spurt of maniacal laughter broke the silence. Kate jerked her head toward the sounds. Her sight was still fuzzy, but good enough to make out the form of a man ... with the flapping wings of a crow on his arm.

The man walked closer and Kate blinked to clear her eyes, her heart crashing in her chest when she recognized him—Damien Darkstone.

Darkstone laughed at the stricken look on Kate's face. "So you *do* remember me."

Kate stared at him. On the surface, he looked like an ordinary man. Dark, straight hair that was worn a little long. Olive skin with a hint of five o'clock shadow on his chin. Black, beady eyes. But Kate knew he was no *ordinary* man— he was a monster who thought nothing of killing anyone who got in his way ... including her.

"What do *you* want?" Kate jerked around in her chair, which barely moved with her effort. It was chained to something. Kate craned her neck to see what it was, her stomach twisting when she realized it was her mother and Sal ... each chained to their own chairs. The three chairs had been linked together with inch-thick steel.

Darkstone stood in front of her, glaring down. The crow, which had moved up to perch on his shoulder, looked down at her too. Kate couldn't help but notice the similarities in their dark, soulless eyes.

"What do I want? Why, you my dear, of course." He gestured toward Carlotta and Sal. "Your friends are just an added bonus."

"But why?" Kate asked.

"Simple." Darkstone fed a piece of something red and gooey to the crow. "I want to make you suffer like you made me suffer when you hunted me relentlessly and put me in prison."

Kate made a face. *Boy this guy really holds a grudge*, she thought as she considered all the trouble he went through to get her here. "I was just doing my job."

"A job you will soon regret having," Darkstone said.

"You're a little too late on that," Kate muttered as she noticed movement behind him. She craned her neck to see what it was, her eyebrows shooting up when she recognized the giant guard from the ice museum.

He grunted at her and shoved his hand up, presumably to show her the missing pinkie finger. Kate grimaced—he looked pretty mad about it.

"Oh, where are my manners?" Darkstone half-waved his hand toward the giant. "Kate, I believe you already know Sheldon."

Kate nodded and Sheldon let out a string of expletives describing Kate in a most derogatory manner before starting toward her. Bloodstone shot his arm out to hold him back and the crow flapped its wings to regain purchase. Kate's heart pounded in her chest, her gaze flickering toward the big red orb Sheldon held in his other hand—the Millennia Ruby.

Bloodstone caught her gaze. "Ahh, yes. The ruby. As you might have guessed, the whole theft was a ruse."

"A ruse? But why?" Kate alternated her gaze between the ruby and Darkstone.

"To lure you here, of course," Darkstone said. "When I heard of the ruby's theft and discovered it was going to be auctioned off in Antarctica, I knew it was the perfect way to get you to come to me."

Kate raised a brow at him while she tested the strength of the chain.

Darkstone paced around the cave as he continued. "I knew I had to be very clever if I wanted to get anywhere near you. And I also knew you would hunt the ruby down with the same overzealous tenacity you hunted me down." He stopped in front of Kate. "So, all I had to do was to steal the ruby myself and then leave a trail of breadcrumbs for you to follow. Naturally, I had Sheldon to help me relieve Crowder of the real ruby and put the fake one in its place."

"So Sheldon helped Summers steal the real one?" Kate felt a momentary satisfaction. She *knew* someone on the inside had helped Summers.

Darkstone nodded. "How very astute of you. The timing was rather risky, though. I had to make sure Summers stole it before you did. I would have been quite upset if you'd gotten to it first. That would have ruined my whole plan."

"But why did you chase me the next day when I stole the fake?"

"We knew you would steal it. So I had a two-pronged plan. One was to get you during your escape, knock you out with tranquilizers then bring you here. Everyone would think Crowder did it and no one would think to trace it to me."

"But that didn't work."

"No." Darkstone frowned. "So we put plan B into action."

"And you killed Summers."

"He was expendable."

"But how did you know I would find the video of him and Benedetti?"

"I didn't. But I left a couple of clues to lead you to Benedetti. The video just happened to be the first one you found."

Kate bristled. *There were other clues she'd missed?*

"Well, you sure seem to have gone to a lot of trouble."

"It was all necessary. I knew if I made the chase too easy, you'd catch on. It *was* a lot of trouble ... and expense." Darkstone smiled at her, an evil smile that didn't make it to his eyes. "But well worth it."

"That seems like a heck of a lot of work when you could have just knocked me out or snuck into my house, grabbed me and brought me here."

Darkstone's forehead wrinkled. "Oh Kate, that sounds so barbaric. Plus if that happened, then someone would soon miss you and start a search. This way you came on your own and I have more time to watch you suffer since no one will be coming to rescue you for a while."

Except her father, Gertie and Frankie, Kate thought. *Surely, by now they would have discovered what happened at the yacht and maybe even gotten in touch with Gideon?*

"Oh, I know about your father and the other old people," Darkstone said as if he could read Kate's mind. "But don't count on them to help you—I have a plan to keep them at bay, and even if by some miracle they reach the top of the volcano intact, they'll be in no condition to help you escape."

Darkstone let out a high-pitched laugh as he stroked the crow's feathers. Kate's blood froze in her veins.

What was Darkstone planning to do to her father ... and to her?

"I have an army of black feathered friends to help me. Don't I?" Darkstone asked the crow on his shoulder who let out a loud screech. Darkstone lifted his arm and jerked his head toward Kate who let out a screech of her own as the crow flew at her, stabbing the tip of its beak into the top of her head before flying back to roost on Darkstone's shoulder.

"Ouch!" Kate screwed her face up at Darkstone. "You trained the crows?"

"They seemed to take to me." He shrugged. "I have a whole army of them waiting to stop anyone that tries to come here."

Kate chewed her bottom lip. Darkstone was even crazier than she'd thought. And more dangerous. She had to figure out a way to get out of this.

"So you didn't even *want* the ruby?" Kate asked. Her mind was clearing now and she figured keeping Darkstone talking was a good way to buy time while she worked on an escape plan.

"Not really." Darkstone took the stone from Sheldon and held it up to the light, staring into its depths. "Oh, I guess I can always use the money, but the real reason I took it was as bait."

"What do you plan to do to me, then?" Kate asked.

"Oh, I plan to watch you squirm in the knowledge of the horrible fate that awaits you."

"Horrible fate?"

"Yes, didn't your nerdy friend tell you? The volcano is about to erupt." Darkstone backed up to the mouth of the cave, which Kate now saw was really more of a cliff. She could see a wall of stone opposite it, but the mouth of the cave itself seemed to drop off. To where she didn't know, but judging by what Darkstone was saying, she was starting to get a pretty good idea.

"Volcano?"

"Can't you see it? Smell it? Hear it?" Darkstone craned his neck over the edge and Kate shivered even though the temperature had grown unbearably warm inside the cave. Warm *and* smelly, like sulfur … or lava.

Her stomach sank like a rock when a strange rumble vibrated the floor of the cave. It was then that she realized they must be inside the mouth of the volcano—the cave a mere opening on the side of the main shaft. She was willing to bet, if she looked over the edge where Darkstone was looking right now, she'd see molten lava bubbling below. Lava that would soon come shooting up out of the shaft and flood the cave where she sat.

Darkstone turned back from the edge and pierced her with his beady eyes. "I'd love to stay and see the look on your face as the molten lava burns your flesh. Will you scream? I think so." He laughed again—that high-pitched crazy person's laugh. "But, as the time for your painful and untimely death draws near, I fear I must bid my final adieu … because I sure as hell don't want to get incinerated by this thing."

"Don't you think you're taking this revenge thing a little too far?" Kate asked. "I mean all I did was arrest you. It's not like I left you to die in hot lava."

"No one crosses Damien Darkstone and lives to tell about it!" Darkstone turned to Sheldon who had been shuffling his feet near the corner. "Is the helicopter ready?"

Sheldon's face crumbled and he looked down at his fee. "Uhh ... That's why I came, Boss. There's a problem you gotta see."

"What problem?" Fury passed across Darkstone's face, but he quickly regained control. "Never mind. I'll see for myself." He turned to Kate. "In the meantime, we'll let Ms. Diamond stew. Don't worry though, Kate. I'll be back to say good-bye."

"I can hardly wait!" Kate yelled after him as he and Sheldon ducked through a small opening in the rock. Kate eyed the crack—it looked to be the only way out. Well, other than going over the edge, which she assumed might be hazardous to their health.

"Mom, Sal ... are you guys okay?" Worry gnawed at Kate—her mother and Sal had been unnervingly quiet during Kate's conversation and she prayed they were okay.

"I'm fine," Carlotta said.

"Me too," Sal added.

"We've found through experience that it's often better just to pretend you're still out in these types of situations." Carlotta wiggled around in her chair, testing the lock and chain that bound her there. "You can usually learn a lot that way."

"And it gives you time to come up with a plan," Sal added.

"So, do you have a plan?" Kate asked wondering just how many times her mother and Sal and been captured and chained up.

"Sure, we get out of these chains, then pretend like we're still chained up." Sal rattled the chains around his wrist. "Then, when Darkstone and that giant come back, we let them get up close to us, capture them by surprise and use them as human shields while we make our escape, using the same opening they came in through."

"That's your plan?" Kate asked incredulously. "How are we going to get out of the chains? In case you haven't noticed, they are solid steel."

"Like this," Sal said and then Kate heard a click and the sound of metal on metal.

"What was that?" Kate twisted her body around to see and then she remembered. Sal's prosthetic thumb—the one Gideon had retrofitted like a Swiss army knife. "Your thumb?"

Sal chuckled. "Yep, and since we're all pretty good lock pickers, I figure between the three of us we should be able to twist ourselves around and use my thumb to pick each one of these locks."

"That's brilliant!" Kate said then her heartbeat kicked into high gear as she glanced at the gap Darkstone had disappeared through. *Did she hear footsteps approaching?*

"We better hurry. He could come back at any minute."

***

Kate tried to sit still in the metal chair and ignore her racing heart. Once they'd freed themselves of the chains, she'd wanted to just sneak out, but Carlotta and Sal had advised against it. According to them, it was much better to wait for Darkstone to come back and try to capture him. Once they did, they could force him to call off his minions. According to them, they'd have a higher chance of things going in their favor and, since Kate had very little experience with being chained to a chair inside a volcano, she decided to take their advice.

So, there she was. In the metal chair, the chains wrapped around as if they were secured. Waiting for Darkstone.

She tapped her finger nervously on her thigh. "What if he does—"

"Shhh," Carlotta whispered. "I think I hear him."

Darkstone appeared at the entrance, a smirk on his face, crow on his shoulder and the Millennia Ruby in his hand.

"Ahhh, I see you are all awake now. I hope you all weren't too uncomfortable awaiting your fate." He looked at them with mock sincerity, fanning himself as he looked over the edge. "I do think it's getting hotter in here, don't you?"

Kate's muscles were tense, but she sat as still as she could, waiting for Sal's signal. The plan was to rush Darkstone when he least expected it. They'd need to execute it flawlessly and had agreed on a signal that would keep them in sync as they launched into action.

But then Kate looked at Darkstone with the ruby. She didn't like the way he was holding it over the edge. Taunting her with it.

"It looks like things are really heating up down there. I guess I'll have to leave soon, though I did want to watch you squirm just a bit more." He looked at the ruby in his hand. "I'll take this with me ... no sense in letting it get liquefied in the lava along with you."

Kate felt anger bubble up inside her. She thought about all the trouble that she'd gone through to find the ruby. How she didn't want to let Max down. And how she *had* to show Ace Mason and the entire FBI that she was good enough to bring the ruby back.

She had too much invested in this to let Darkstone take the ruby now.

Without another thought, Kate shrugged off the chains and launched herself from the chair toward Darkstone, relishing the look of surprise in his eyes and ignoring her mother's panicked cries.

She felt a smug satisfaction as the force of her body smacked into Darkstone's with a thud. She grabbed on to the ruby, closed her eyes and said a silent prayer as they both fell over the cliff into the depths of the volcano.

Chapter Twenty Six

A rush of hot air blew Kate's hair back from her face. Her stomach swooped with weightlessness. Darkstone's screams mingling with her own and the caw of the crow, that was flapping downward alongside Darkstone, vibrated in her ears.

She tucked the ruby under her arm like a quarterback running for the goalpost as she fell. Darkstone was falling at the same speed only a few feet away from her and Kate thought the look of incredulousness in his eyes was almost worth plunging to her fiery death.

But Kate didn't have to plunge to a fiery death. She had one last ace in the hole that Darkstone didn't know about. They'd taken away her wrist communicator, climbing gloves and cell phone, but left on her vest. And that vest wasn't just any vest. As usual, Gideon had equipped it with a special gadget. Kate reached for the string at the top of the vest, said a silent prayer and tugged.

The glider wings shot out from the side of the vest slowing her freefall. She was still close enough to Darkstone to see his face fill with rage. He reached out toward her, as if she would save him. But she didn't. Instead, she watched as he fell further away.

Kate searched the walls of the volcano shaft frantically for a cave, ledge or even a jagged piece of rock sticking out where she could land. Spotting a shallow ledge, she used the strings on the vest to guide herself over to it. She managed to land without a hitch, thankful she'd paid attention when Gideon had demonstrated how to use the vest earlier that year.

Hot, acrid air burned her lungs as she looked down into the shaft. Darkstone was just a mere speck now but she could still hear him. Then, just as he disappeared from view, the crow screeched an eerie sound that echoed off the walls and rattled her bones. Seconds later, she heard flapping and cawing from above as dozens of crows dived into the shaft, following Darkstone.

"Kate, are you okay?"

Kate looked up. Her mother was standing about twenty feet up at the mouth of the cave on the opposite side of the shaft, looking down at her.

"Fine." Kate waved. "I just have to figure out a way to climb up."

"If you can work your way around to this side, we'll lower down the chains," Sal said.

"But what if Darkstone's henchmen come? It might be better if you guys act like you are still chained up."

"And leave you hanging down there?" Carlotta made a face. "No way."

Kate looked down at her feet. She still wore the rock climbing shoes Gideon had sent. They had metal picks embedded inside that jutted out of the front of the shoe by pressing a button hidden on the side. Studded cleats shot out of the bottom at the press of another button.

Looking up at the rock wall, Kate could see it was loaded with fissures and small ledges. She could fashion spikes from the carbon fiber rods in the hang glider wings on the vest and work her way up just like any other rock climbing expedition. She'd rock climbed hundreds of times. This should be a piece of cake.

"I think it will be easier for me—" Kate was cut short by a strange noise.

Thwack. Thwack. Thwack.

"Do you hear that?" she asked. She didn't need their answer. She could tell Carlotta and Sal heard it by the way they cocked their heads toward the top of the cone.

The sound, which seemed familiar, was getting louder. It was coming from outside the cone of the volcano. Kate's heart stalled as she recognized what it was—Darkstone's helicopter.

Kate wasn't sure what might happen if Darkstone's crew found her in this position, but she was pretty sure it wouldn't be anything good. She was too exposed and too vulnerable to any kind of attack. Sheldon was still pretty pissed off about his finger and she could picture the look of glee on his face as he shot her and sent her flailing into the abyss that she'd just dispatched Darkstone into.

She had no doubt that Sheldon would finish her off ... but only if he could *see* her. She motioned for her mother and Sal to get back as she looked around frantically for a crevice that she could squirm into.

Spotting one on the right, she quickly maneuvered her way over. Sucking in her breath, she squeezed into the small space, praying that nothing stuck out enough for them to notice.

The helicopter sounds grew louder. Kate felt her heart thudding to the rhythm of the blades as she held her breath and waited.

"Kate! Carlie!" Though distorted by the echo in the volcano shaft, the voice had a familiar ring to it.

She took a risk, peeking out from her hiding place and looking up into the opening at the top of the shaft where the helicopter hovered. The side door was open and a man leaned out dangerously.

Kate's heart surged as she looked up at the familiar form.

"Dad?"

***

Vic lowered himself on a rescue cable to collect Kate while Carlotta and Sal took the less scenic route of simply leaving through the cave exit. There was no risk of them running into any of Darkstone's minions since, according to Vic, they had all been captured.

"But how did you know we were inside the volcano?" Kate asked as she and Vic unhooked themselves inside the helicopter.

"Once we captured Darkstone's minions, it was pretty easy to get them to talk."

The familiar voice came from the pilot and Kate whipped her head in that direction, her stomach doing a strange series of flip-flops when her eyes confirmed her suspicion. The pilot was Ace Mason.

"What are *you* doing here?" Kate's narrow-eyed gaze ping-ponged from her father to Ace. Last she knew, the two men barely got along in the same room, never mind coordinating a rescue mission inside a helicopter.

"I figured out you'd given me the slip back at the hotel, then found out you'd come to this island. So I hired a boat and came over," Ace said.

"He got here right about the time Gertie, Frankie, and I were forming a rescue party to get you, your mother and Sal," Vic added.

"So you knew about Blue Crow Island?" Kate asked.

"Not exactly." Ace grimaced. "Gideon told me."

"Gideon *told* you?" *The traitor.*

Ace sighed. "When I realized you'd given us the slip, I panicked. I knew Darkstone was behind all this ..."

"What?" Anger bubbled up in Kate's chest.

He knew all along and didn't tell her?

"Kate, I'm sorry I should have told you from the beginning, but that information was restricted to FBI personnel involved in the case only." Ace glanced back at her sheepishly. "In my defense, I did try to get you to back off several times ..."

Kate's mouth flew open but she was too furious to string words together in a coherent sentence. Ace Mason hadn't changed a bit. He was still the "do it by the book no matter what" FBI guy that cared more about FBI rules than anything.

"Anyway," Ace continued, "when I realized you'd slipped away and could be walking into one of Darkstone's traps, I called Gideon. He'd just witnessed your abduction, so he felt it was best to fill us in so we could come and rescue you."

Rescue her?

Kate's hands balled into fists and she marched over to Ace who looked at her fearfully as he tried to land the plane.

"Hey, wait a minute." Kate jabbed her index finger in his direction. "I didn't need *rescuing*. I could have climbed out of that volcano just fine on my own. *And*, to top it off, I had to do *your* job and get rid of the bad guy!"

"Now, now," Vic soothed as he pulled Kate over to him and kissed the top of her head. "Everything worked out for the best, Kitten. We wouldn't have been able to capture Darkstone's people if we didn't have the added help of the FBI."

Kate doubted that. She felt certain they could have pulled it off without Ace Mason or any other FBI help, but the helicopter jolted to a landing and they were rushed by Carlotta and the others before she got a chance to say so.

The next thing Kate knew, she was in the middle of a round of hugging with everyone gushing about how great it was they were all alive. Eventually she found herself facing Ace Mason, who grabbed her in a hug before she had a chance to protest.

It must have been the excitement. When Ace's arms went around her, Kate felt a rush of emotion. She felt safe. Secure. She started to melt into his embrace, her heartbeat kicking into high gear and her insides starting to get all tingly. She was still clutching the Millennia Ruby and she felt his hand snake around her waist toward it.

Kate jerked back, flattening her left palm on Ace's chest and pushing him away while she clutched the ruby tighter with her right hand.

"Oh no ... you're not getting the ruby," she said.

Ace spread his hands at his sides. "I wasn't trying to get the ruby, Kate."

Kate glanced sideways at him. He almost sounded like he meant it.

"Hey, we better get going," Vic yelled. "The volcano could blow at any moment."

Kate's stomach twisted as she looked at the gray smoke billowing from the top of the volcano.

"I'll take the bad guys back in the helicopter." Ace pointed to the left then turned to Vic. "You guys take the boats."

"Okay," Vic said, then did something that made Kate's jaw drop. He clapped Ace on the back and said, "Good job, son."

Son?

Kate stared at them as they shook hands, looking at each other with something Kate thought she'd never see them look at each other with—mutual respect. Carlotta was standing behind Vic. Kate caught her eye and made a face while she tilted her head toward the two men.

Carlotta shrugged. Apparently, Vic and Ace had formed some sort of bond during the rescue. Kate just hoped that didn't mean they'd be inviting him over for holiday dinners.

As the two continued with their bonding ritual, Kate's gaze drifted to the left where Ace had pointed. Four men were chained up with what looked like the very chains that had held her, Carlotta and Sal. One of them was Sheldon. Their eyes locked and he shoved his pinkie-less hand up in a gesture that was reminiscent of giving one the bird. Except in his case, it was four fingers and no pinkie.

"How do you know Darkstone is dead?" Ace pulled her attention away from Sheldon.

"I pushed him into the shaft of the volcano," Kate said. "I watched him fall."

"You're sure he's dead?" Ace glanced uncertainly at the volcano.

"Of course, no one could survive a fall like that, could they?"

"Well, you did."

Kate frowned. "Yeah, but I had special equipment. I *saw* him fall all the way down. And my mother and Sal did, too."

"Okay," Ace said. "You're right. He must be dead in there."

A man approached them. "Ace, we better get going."

"Kate, this is my new partner, Mick." Kate's eyes widened. So *this* was who had replaced her. She murmured a greeting and the two of them shook hands, then Ace tossed a set of keys to Mick. "Jim and I will take the captives in the helicopter and you take the boat back."

Mick nodded and headed off.

Ace turned back to Kate. She saw emotion flood his eyes and he reached out almost as if to touch her, then let his hand fall back to his side. "You'll have to come in to headquarters and give a statement."

"Of course," Kate said feeling a little disappointed that he hadn't touched her. She didn't want him to though, did she?

"Okay, I guess I'll see you there, then." Ace turned and walked away.

Kate stared after him feeling ... well, she didn't know exactly *what* she was feeling.

"Katie. Come on! We gotta get out of here!" Vic's voice interrupted her thoughts and she turned and hurried after her father, the sound of the helicopter taking off drumming in her ears.

As they walked back to the beach, Carlotta recounted the details of their capture and how

Kate pushed Darkstone into the volcano. Vic filled them in on how he, Gertie and Frankie had teamed up with the FBI. Everyone, except the two FBI guys, got a good laugh out of that—no one ever thought any of the *Golden Capers* gang would be working *with* the FBI.

They used the inflatable to ferry themselves to their respective boats. The FBI were nice enough to hang around while Sal spliced together the electrical wires that had been cut during the abduction, even though Kate did catch them glancing uneasily at the volcano, which was starting to emit louder and more frequent rumblings.

Once power was restored to the *High Jinx*, the two boats took off, leaving the grumbling, bubbling volcano in their wake.

"Is the satellite connection restored?" Kate slid into the dinette and placed the Millennia Ruby on the table.

"It is," Carlotta said as she picked the ruby up and held it to the shattered window. The sunlight filtered into the crystal lighting it with a deep red glow. "Now *this* is more like it."

Kate couldn't wait to call into the museum and let them know she had the ruby. *Should she call Max's private line or the lab?*

On the one hand, she *was* kind of mad at Gideon for telling Ace about the island but she had to admit the presence of the four extra FBI guys *had* tipped the scales in their favor. Plus, Gideon's glider vest and switchblade thumb had saved the day.

She brought up Skype and pressed the button to call the lab.

"Kate. Are you all right?" Gideon's worried voice blared out of the computer.

"Is that Kate?" Kate practically melted as she heard Max's voice. "Kate—I've been so worried about you."

She stared at the screen, which showed an empty lab. Where was everyone? Or Max in particular ... she could see Gideon any time. As if on cue, Gideon's face filled the screen. His hair was a disheveled mess and his forehead creased with worry.

"I'm fine," Kate said. "Are you okay? You look like crap."

"I've been worried about *you*!" Gideon said.

"Well, no need to worry. The bad guys have been taken care of ... and I have something to bring back." Kate proudly held the Millennia Ruby in front of her so they could see it back at the lab.

"You got the ruby?" Gideon asked.

"Yes," Kate said. "Why don't you move out of the way and let Max see it?" *Or let me see Max.*

Kate held her breath as Gideon's face zoomed away and was replaced by a large blue mass. Squinting at the screen, Kate realized it was the crotch of someone's pants. Max's pants ... he was standing in front of the computer!

"I hear you went above and beyond the call of duty to get that," Max's voice said. "Gideon tells me that crazy killer, Darkstone, did all this to lure you to him."

"Yep, but I took care of him *and* got the ruby," Kate said. "Have a seat and I'll hold it up closer so you can see it's the real deal."

Kate felt her cheeks turn red as she watched the crotch on the computer screen move. Max's crotch. It was nice and all, but she really wanted to see the rest of him. She held her breath, waiting for his face to come on the screen.

Instead, she saw a tanned arm lightly dotted with dark hair and wearing a Rolex watch.

"I wish I could stay and talk, but I have a meeting." Max moved away from the computer and Kate saw a view of the lab again. "I just came down to keep Gideon company as he was frantic with worry. But now that you're okay, I must tend to business. We'll catch up when you get back."

"Right, of course," Kate said hiding her disappointment.

Ka Boom!

The explosion, even as far away as it was, rocked the boat and Kate had to hold on to the table to keep from falling over.

"What the devil was that?" Max's voice again, laced with concern.

Kate looked behind her. In the distance, she could see Blue Crow Island ... or what was left of it. The top of the volcano had been blown clear off and there was a cloud of debris above it. Glowing red lava poured down the sides toward the island below. Kate shuddered—even if Darkstone had somehow survived the fall, he certainly couldn't have survived *that*.

"That," she said, "was the end of Blue Crow Island ... and Damien Darkstone."

"Let's see." Gideon's eager face filled the screen and Kate turned her computer so that the camera could capture the island.

"I must commend you on a job well done," Max said. "You killed a violent criminal, captured his henchmen and escaped an exploding island, all to bring the Millennia Ruby back home to the museum."

Kate's heart surged as she basked in the glow of Max's praise.

"Thanks," she said. Then, so as not to appear too full of herself, she shrugged and added. "It's all in a day's work."

"I'm glad you feel that way," Max replied. "I was afraid you might ask for a raise."

Chapter Twenty Seven

Two days later, Kate stood on the steps of the FBI building after a grueling six-hour interview where she'd told the same story about what happened in the volcano with Darkstone over and over again to several different agents.

"I guess you guys really want to make sure Darkstone's dead, huh?" Kate said to Ace, who had escorted her out of the building and was now standing on the steps beside her.

Ace shrugged. "We never recovered a body."

"You expected a body? The man was incinerated."

Ace laughed. "I know, but you know how the bureau likes to cross its t's and dot its i's."

"There's just one thing," Kate said. "How did you know so much about the ruby theft?"

Ace smiled. "We're the FBI. We have our ways."

Kate's thoughts drifted to the man she'd thought looked familiar at the hotel—Westlake. "You had someone inside the ice hotel, didn't you?"

Ace shrugged.

"Wait a minute." Kate narrowed her eyes at him. "Were you planning on stealing the ruby from there too?"

Ace shook his head. "No. Of course not. It was never about the ruby anyway, Kate. It was always about keeping you safe."

Kate stared into his eyes. He seemed sincere, but she didn't know if she believed him.

Finally, she broke eye contact and glanced down the street. Max had said he was going to pick her up in his Ferrari Testerosa and take her to *Clio,* one of the best French restaurants in Boston, to celebrate the return of the Millennia Ruby.

"So anyway, I was hoping we could bury the hatchet and you'd let me buy you a burger and a beer," Ace said.

Kate whipped her head back in his direction. She had to admit he looked kind of cute standing there with his hands in his pockets, shuffling his feet on the ground. He seemed nervous about her answer and for some reason that tugged at her heart.

Did he really want to be friends again ... or was this just a ruse to get close to her so he could get information on the next case?

"Well, I ..." Kate stammered. She wasn't sure what she wanted to do. She was finally going to get to see what Max looked like. *And* he was going to pick her up in a Ferrari and take her to a fancy restaurant. Surely, that was more appealing than a burger and beer with Ace Mason.

She glanced back down the street, then back at Ace. He had a boyish, hopeful look on his face that made him very appealing. She bit her bottom lip and saw something flash in the depths of his gray eyes.

Her stomach flip-flopped like a teenager, but her heart didn't follow. She wasn't ready to forgive Ace Mason yet. She didn't know if she'd ever be ready.

Looking down the street again, she saw the red Ferrari turn the corner.

"Sorry, Ace. Max is coming to pick me up." She nodded toward the car that was pulling to the curb, its dark windows making it impossible to see inside. She ran around to the passenger side.

"Oh." Ace's face hardened. "Well, maybe some other time then."

"Sure." Kate smiled over the hood of the car at him as she opened the passenger door. "Some other time."

The smell of "new car" and leather tickled Kate's nose as she slid into the buttery black leather seat. Her stomach fluttered with anticipation. She slowly turned her head and looked straight into the deep, brown eyes of … Mercedes LaChance.

"You?" What are you doing here?"

"Max had some business but he let us take the car," Gideon said as he stuck his head in-between the two seats. Kate craned her neck to look behind her and noticed Gideon's body uncomfortably wedged on the luggage shelf behind the front seats.

"And use the expense account." Mercedes waved a credit card in Kate's face as she pulled out into traffic.

"He said we could buy ourselves a great meal and maybe see a show," Gideon added, "as a reward for our fine work in getting the ruby back."

Kate cut her eyes over to Mercedes. "Well, I know what Gideon did and what I did, but what did *you* do?"

"Come on Kate, you know I keep everything running like a greased wheel," Mercedes said.

Kate made a face. As far as she was concerned, Mercedes was more of a hindrance than a help.

"Yeah like getting these photos of Blue Crow Island." Gideon shoved some photos between the seats. They showed an ash covered island with a big volcano sticking out of the middle.

"That's what it looks like now?" Kate's brow creased. All the lush vegetation was gone—covered with ash and rock.

"Yes." Gideon pushed the glasses up on his nose. "It's all rock now. Not one single Blue Crow survived—It's such a shame the whole species is extinct."

"You know this case was kind of weird," Kate said. "It started with Crowder, 'The Crow", and ended with a bunch of weird crows on an island."

"At least you got two good things out of it—you got rid of Darkstone, and you got the ruby back," Gideon said.

"Yeah, all in all it came out pretty good," Kate replied. She relaxed into her seat as Mercedes zigzagged through the traffic. It had worked out pretty good. Kate felt satisfied that she'd proven herself to Max and redeemed herself in the eyes of the FBI. *And* the fact that she'd never have to worry about Darkstone again was an added bonus.

Plop.

"Eww, what's that?" Mercedes fumbled around on the steering wheel for the knob that worked the wipers.

Kate stared at the large white blob that had appeared on the windshield, her stomach growing uneasy as she realized it was bird poop. Something in the middle of the white blob caught her eye and she bolted up in her seat.

"Hey is that a bl—"

Mercedes found the wipers and they squeegeed across the window obliterating the bird poop and the bright blue downy feather that Kate *thought* she'd seen right smack in the middle of it.

"What?" Gideon asked.

"Nothing," Kate said as she sank back into the seat pushing the image of the feather from her mind. Plenty of birds had bright blue feathers, didn't they?

She'd been hoping for a night out with Max, but now it looked like she was going to get Mercedes, Gideon and bird poop. With a sigh, she glanced out at the shops and restaurants whizzing by. She'd make the best of it, relax and enjoy a night filled with fun and free of trouble.

That's why Kate didn't want to think about the feather or where it might have come from. She knew that would be inviting trouble to find her and, from her experience, trouble didn't need an invitation—it always had a way of knowing exactly where she was.

The end.

About The Author

Leighann Dobbs discovered her passion for writing after a twenty year career as a software engineer. She lives in New Hampshire with her husband Bruce, their trusty Chihuahua mix Mojo and beautiful rescue cat, Kitty. When she's not reading, gardening or selling antiques, she likes to write romance and cozy mystery novels and novelettes which are perfect for the busy person on the go.

Find out about her latest books and how to get discounts on them by signing up at:

http://www.leighanndobbs.com/newsletter

Connect with Leighann on Facebook and Twitter

http://facebook.com/leighanndobbsbooks
http://twitter.com/leighanndobbs

***

More Books By This Author:

Blackmoore Sisters
Paranormal Mystery Series

* * *

Dead Wrong
Dead & Buried
Dead Tide
Buried Secrets

Lexy Baker
Cozy Mystery Series
* * *

Killer Cupcakes
Dying For Danish
Murder, Money and Marzipan
3 Bodies and a Biscotti
Brownies, Bodies & Bad Guys
Bake, Battle & Roll
Wedded Blintz

Contemporary
Romance
* * *

Sweet Escapes
Reluctant Romance

Dobbs "Fancytales"
Regency Romance Fairytales Series
* * *

Something In Red
Snow White and the Seven Rogues
Dancing On Glass
The Beast of Edenmaine
The Reluctant Princess

A Note From The Author

I hope you enjoyed reading this book as much as I enjoyed writing it. This is the first book in the Kate Diamond Adventure series and I have a whole bunch more planned!

If you like this adventure, you might like my Blackmoore Sister's series. I have an excerpt from book One *"Dead Wrong"* at the end of this book.

This book has been through many edits with several people and even some software programs, but since nothing is infallible (even the software programs) you might catch a spelling error or mistake and, if you do, I sure would appreciate it if you let me know - you can contact me at *lee@leighanndobbs.com*.

Oh, and I love to connect with my readers so please do visit me on facebook at *http://www.facebook.com/leighanndobbsbooks* or at my website *http://www.leighanndobbs.com*.

Are you signed up to get notifications of my latest releases and special contests? Go to: *http://www.leighanndobbs.com/newsletter* and enter your email address to signup - I promise never to share it and I only send emails every couple of weeks so I won't fill up your inbox.

Excerpt From Dead Wrong:

Morgan Blackmoore tapped her finger lightly on the counter, her mind barely registering the low buzz of voices behind her in the crowded coffee shop as she mentally prioritized the tasks that awaited her back at her own store.

"Here you go, one yerba mate tea and a vanilla latte." Felicity rang up the purchase, as Morgan dug in the front pocket of her faded denim jeans for some cash which she traded for the two paper cups.

Inhaling the spicy aroma of the tea, she turned to leave, her long, silky black hair swinging behind her. Elbowing her way through the crowd, she headed toward the door. At this time of morning, the coffee shop was filled with locals and Morgan knew almost all of them well enough to exchange a quick greeting or nod.

Suddenly a short, stout figure appeared, blocking her path. Morgan let out a sharp breath, recognizing the figure as Prudence Littlefield.

Prudence had a long running feud with the Blackmoore's which dated back to some sort of run-in she'd had with Morgan's grandmother when they were young girls. As a result, Prudence loved to harass and berate the Blackmoore girls in public. Morgan's eyes darted around the room, looking for an escape route.

"Just who do you think you are?" Prudence demanded, her hands fisted on her hips, legs spaced shoulder width apart. Morgan noticed she was wearing her usual knee high rubber boots and an orange sunflower scarf.

Morgan's brow furrowed over her ice blue eyes as she stared at the older woman's prune like face.

"Excuse me?"

"Don't you play dumb with me Morgan Blackmoore. What kind of concoction did you give my Ed? He's been acting plumb crazy."

Morgan thought back over the previous week's customers. Ed Littlefield *had* come into her herbal remedies shop, but she'd be damned if she'd announce to the whole town what he was after.

She narrowed her eyes at Prudence. "That's between me and Ed."

Prudence's cheeks turned crimson. Her nostrils flared. "You know what *I* think," she said narrowing her eyes and leaning in toward Morgan, "I think you're a witch, just like your great-great-great-grandmother!"

Morgan felt an angry heat course through her veins. There was nothing she hated more than being called a witch. She was a Doctor of Pharmacology with a Master Herbalist's license, not some sort of spell-casting conjurer.

The coffee shop had grown silent. Morgan could feel the crowd staring at her. She leaned forward, looking wrinkled old Prudence Littlefield straight in the eye.

"Well now, I think we know that's not true," she said, her voice barely above a whisper, "Because if I was a witch, I'd have turned you into a newt long ago."

Then she pushed her way past the old crone and fled out the coffee shop door.

***

Fiona Blackmoore stared at the amethyst crystal in front of her wondering how to work it into a pendant. On most days, she could easily figure out exactly how to cut and position the stone, but right now her brain was in a pre-caffeine fog.

Where was Morgan with her latte?

She sighed, looking at her watch. It was ten past eight, Morgan should be here by now, she thought impatiently.

Fiona looked around the small shop, *Sticks and Stones*, she shared with her sister. An old cottage that had been in the family for generations, it sat at one of the highest points in their town of Noquitt, Maine.

Turning in her chair, she looked out the back window. In between the tree trunks that made up a small patch of woods, she had a bird's eye view of the sparkling, sapphire blue Atlantic Ocean in the distance.

The cottage sat about 500 feet inland at the top of a high cliff that plunged into the Atlantic. If the woods were cleared, like the developers wanted, the view would be even better. But Fiona would have none of that, no matter how much the developers offered them, or how much they needed the money. She and her sisters would never sell the cottage.

She turned away from the window and surveyed the inside of the shop. One side was setup as an apothecary of sorts. Antique slotted shelves loaded with various herbs lined the walls. Dried weeds hung from the rafters and several mortar and pestles stood on the counter, ready for whatever herbal concoctions her sister was hired to make.

On her side sat a variety of gemologist tools and a large assortment of crystals. Three antique oak and glass jewelry cases displayed her creations. Fiona smiled as she looked at them. Since childhood she had been fascinated with rocks and gems so it was no surprise to anyone when she grew up to become a gemologist and jewelry designer, creating jewelry not only for its beauty, but also for its healing properties.

The two sisters vocations suited each other perfectly and they often worked together providing customers with crystal and herbal healing for whatever ailed them.

The jangling of the bell over the door brought her attention to the front of the shop. She breathed a sigh of relief when Morgan burst through the door, her cheeks flushed, holding two steaming paper cups.

"What's the matter?" Fiona held her hand out, accepting the drink gratefully. Peeling back the plastic tab, she inhaled the sweet vanilla scent of the latte.

"I just had a run in with Prudence Littlefield!" Morgan's eyes flashed with anger.

"Oh? I saw her walking down Shore road this morning wearing that god-awful orange sunflower scarf. What was the run-in about this time?" Fiona took the first sip of her latte, closing her eyes and waiting for the caffeine to power her blood stream. She'd had her own run-ins with Pru Littlefield and had learned to take them in stride.

"She was upset about an herbal mix I made for Ed. She called me a witch!"

"What did you make for him?"

"Just some Ginkgo, Ginseng and Horny Goat Weed ... although the latter he said was for Prudence."

Fiona's eyes grew wide. "Aren't those herbs for impotence?"

Morgan shrugged "Well, that's what he wanted."

"No wonder Prudence was mad...although you'd think just being married to her would have caused the impotence."

Morgan burst out laughing. "No kidding. I had to question his sanity when he asked me for it. I thought maybe he had a girlfriend on the side."

Fiona shook her head trying to clear the unwanted images of Ed and Prudence Littlefield together.

"Well, I wouldn't let it ruin my day. You know how *she* is."

Morgan put her tea on the counter, then turned to her apothecary shelf and picked several herbs out of the slots. "I know, but she always seems to know how to push my buttons. Especially when she calls me a witch."

Fiona grimaced. "Right, well I wish we *were* witches. Then we could just conjure up some money and not be scrambling to pay the taxes on this shop and the house."

Morgan sat in a tall chair behind the counter and proceeded to measure dried herbs into a mortar.

"I know. I saw Eli Stark in town yesterday and he was pestering me about selling the shop again."

"What did you tell him?"

"I told him we'd sell over our dead bodies." Morgan picked up a pestle and started grinding away at the herbs.

Fiona smiled. Eli Stark had been after them for almost a year to sell the small piece of land their shop sat on. He had visions of buying it, along with some adjacent lots in order to develop the area into high end condos.

Even though their parents early deaths had left Fiona, Morgan and their two other sisters property rich but cash poor the four of them agreed they would never sell. Both the small shop and the stately ocean home they lived in had been in the family for generations and they didn't want *their* generation to be the one that lost them.

The only problem was, although they owned the properties outright, the taxes were astronomical and, on their meager earnings, they were all just scraping by to make ends meet.

All the more reason to get this necklace finished so I can get paid. Thankfully, the caffeine had finally cleared the cobwebs in her head and Fiona was ready to get to work. Staring down at the amethyst, a vision of the perfect shape to cut the stone appeared in her mind. She grabbed her tools and started shaping the stone.

Fiona and Morgan were both lost in their work. They worked silently, the only sounds in the little shop being the scrape of mortar on pestle and the hum of Fiona's gem grinding tool mixed with a few melodic tweets and chirps that floated in from the open window.

Fiona didn't know how long they were working like that when the bell over the shop door chimed again. She figured it must have been an hour or two judging by the fact that the few sips left in the bottom of her latte cup had grown cold.

She smiled, looking up from her work to greet their potential customer, but the smile froze on her face when she saw who it was.

Sheriff Overton stood in the door flanked by two police officers. A toothpick jutted out of the side of Overton's mouth and judging by the looks on all three of their faces, they weren't there to buy herbs or crystals.

Fiona could almost hear her heart beating in the silence as the men stood there, adjusting their eyes to the light and getting their bearings.

"Can we help you?" Morgan asked, stopping her work to wipe her hands on a towel.

Overton's head swiveled in her direction like a hawk spying a rabbit in a field.

"That's her." He nodded to the two uniformed men who approached Morgan hesitantly. Fiona recognized one of the men as

Brody Hunter, whose older brother Morgan had dated all through high school. She saw Brody look questioningly at the Sheriff.

The other man stood a head taller than Brody. Fiona noticed his dark hair and broad shoulders but her assessment of him stopped there when she saw him pulling out a pair of handcuffs.

Her heart lurched at the look of panic on her sister's face as the men advanced toward her.

"Just what is this all about?" She demanded, standing up and taking a step toward the Sheriff.

There was no love lost between the Sheriff and Fiona. They'd had a few run-ins and she thought he was an egotistical bore and probably crooked too. He ignored her question focusing his attention on Morgan. The next words out of his mouth chilled Fiona to the core.

"Morgan Blackmoore ... you're under arrest for the murder of Prudence Littlefield."

***

Visit *http://www.leighanndobbs.com* to find out where you can buy *Dead Wrong*.

39332051R00174

Made in the USA
Lexington, KY
18 February 2015